MY SECRET AFFAIR WITH THE TRILLIONAIRE

A Futuristic Valentines Romance

M.M. Wakeford

Preface

This story is set sometime in the future, in the same universe as my sci-fi novels Krantor's Mate and Melinda's Choice. Although we meet again some of the characters in those books, this novella is completely standalone. There are scenes of an explicit sexual nature that make this story unsuitable for anyone under the age of 18.

Chapter 1

Viva

Slowly, I slide my two oiled hands down his body, pushing down with my palms to exert just the right pressure to release the tension. When I reach the small of his back, just above the buttocks, I pause, pressing down gently. He groans. I press down again, this time moving my palms in slow circles, relaxing those muscles that are wound up so tight from sitting at his office chair for too many hours in the day. "That good?" I enquire softly.

"Oh yeah."

I smile. The best part of my job is making people feel good. Here at Sensual Healing, we specialize in deep, sensual massage, harnessing centuries of human knowledge about the body, the mind and the pleasure-giving gift of touch. To become master healers, we must complete a rigorous round of training, and only the best of the best are allowed to practise here at this exclusive, high end establishment.

My hands glide down to his hairy buttocks, kneading those two mounds in a slow, skilful pattern designed to both loosen up muscles and bring about erotic sensation. I let my fingers graze the rosebud of his anus, but I don't linger there, moving on to stroke his perineum then back to his buttocks, repeating the process over and over again. He emits various sounds—grunts, moans, sighs—as he lets go of all the cares that come with his job as a high school principal, and allows himself to drift into a blissful state of being. Mr Johnson has been my client since his wife bought him a treatment package at Sensual Healing as a birthday gift six months ago. Since then, he comes to me once a month without fail, arriving tired and tense, and leaving energized and content. Our services are not cheap, but they are worth every cent.

I spend time on each of his legs, kneading and releasing tension, before giving his feet special attention, caressing them with my touch and pressing on known points for healing. The flagship Sensual Healing treatment differs according to the needs and preferences of the client, but in all cases it begins with an immersive dip in the hot spa bath, which contains a proprietary blend of healing essences, followed by a sensual, full body massage which culminates in orgasmic bliss—what some would call a "happy ending". However, we do not like to use such terms here. Loni, the owner and manager of Sensual Healing, is very clear on what we are as an establishment, and what we are not.

Although sex work has been legal and regulated in this state for the past decade, we are not sex workers. At all times, master healers remain fully dressed. We may use intimate touch to bring about a state of intense relaxation and bliss in our clients, but that is as far as it goes. We maintain a high standard of professionalism, hygiene and discretion. This is explained clearly and explicitly to all new patrons before they begin their first treatment. Any groping or sexual propositioning of the master healers will result in immediate expulsion, and no refund.

I finish with Mr Johnson's feet and assist him to turn onto his back. I ensure he is comfortably situated before I begin to massage the front of his body. My hands glide smoothly over his chest and pot belly, taking time to stimulate his nipples with a few light pinches along the way. His stubby cock is stiff, a little precum glistening at the bulbous tip. All in good time, I smile to myself. He'll get to come, but not before I edge him with my sensuous touch over every inch of his body.

Through my work at Sensual Healing these past three years, I have treated people of all shapes, sizes and gender. I have seen and touched all parts of their bodies. To say I have become inured to the sight of aroused genitals may not be an exaggeration. While I have appreciated my fair share of cocks, pussies and asses in my time, for the most part, this is work for me, not pleasure. Of course, I derive tremendous satisfaction from making my clients feel good, but it's hardly the panty wetting type of satisfaction. This job is safe, respectable, well paid and the hours suit me. I'm home most mornings, so I get to have breakfast with my six-year-old, Joe, and to walk him to school. Some days, I'm even able to have enough of a gap between treatments to be there for school pick-ups. On the days when I can't, I'm lucky that my mom steps in to help out.

Today, unfortunately, is one of those days where my schedule has not allowed me to get Joe from school. I glance at the wall clock. He should be home by now. As soon as this treatment is over, I'll give him a call. My hands are now on Mr Johnson's cock, absently stroking the short, thick shaft while my mind wanders elsewhere. I give myself a mental shake. Loni has drilled it into us at countless training workshops that we must be present in our minds at all times during treatments, in order to channel our healing energy. I bring my focus back to Mr Johnson, intent on giving him the utmost ecstasy. With a practised, well-oiled hand, I stroke up and down his shaft while my other hand presses gently on his perineum, stimulating his prostate gland. I summon loving, joyful energy within me and transmit it through my touch. It is this energy, as much as my touch, which brings my clients to orgasmic bliss. I truly believe it.

Beneath my fingers, I feel Mr Johnson's cock swell and jerk. He is close. I step to the side, not stopping the movement of my hands. As protocol dictates, a master healer must keep the appropriate distance so as to ensure face and clothes are not contaminated by any ejaculate. My client grunts, and I bring my fist to the tip of his cock, milking his release, most of which shoots into the palm of my hand. When he is done, I retrieve a wet cloth and clean him up, then wash my hands. I bring a warm blanket and wrap it over Mr Johnson, then finish the treatment with a gentle press of my palms to his feet, grounding him. Softly, I say, "When you are ready, sit up slowly and take all the time you need. Please make sure you do rehydrate; I have left a bottle of water right beside you. I will leave you now to get dressed at your leisure. Thank you for your patronage, Mr Johnson, and I hope to see you again for another treatment soon."

"Thanks, Viva. That was awesome, as usual."

"I'm glad. Go in peace."

I let myself out of the treatment room, closing the door with a quiet click, then head to the staff quarters where I quickly wash my hands and guzzle down some water. Once these immediate necessities are done, I open my locker and take out my communicator. Mom answers on the second ring.

"Hey, Viva," she says with a warm smile. She's sitting at the kitchen table, nursing a hot drink.

"Hey, Mom. How's things?"

"All good, honey. Joe is super excited about his trip to the city farm. He couldn't stop talking about it all the way home. Here, let me call him. Joe! Come speak to your mom."

There is the sound of running feet, then Joe is there, beaming at me. My heart clenches at the sight of him—his wavy brown hair falling haphazardly about his cute little face, his large brown eyes so like mine, and the dimples in his smile. "Mom! I fed the goats. It was so cool. I just held out my hand and they licked the food off me." He giggles. "It tickled!"

"I bet."

"And then we went to see the rabbits and guinea pigs. Ms Davis brought out this fluffy white rabbit and let us stroke it. Can we get a pet rabbit, Mom?"

"Let me think about it, sweet boy. Having pets is a huge responsibility. They need lots of care."

"I promise to take care of it."

"We'll see."

We talk a bit more before I end the call. I need to go prepare for one last client tonight. Quickly, I go to my treatment room, knocking on the door first to make sure Mr Johnson is no longer there. Methodically, I sanitize the room and lay fresh towels on the massage bed. Then I go through to the adjoining bathroom and clean out the spa tub before refilling it with hot water and dropping a cupful of aromatic salts into it. I lay fresh towels there too and a new bath mat, ensuring all is ready for my next client. I feel a little shiver of anticipation. This is not just any client. It's Tobias Moore.

Yes, that Tobias Moore, the self-made trillionaire who regularly tops the Forbes list. For two years now, he has had a standing appointment with me every Friday at six pm. It beggars belief that someone as rich and powerful as him comes here to get a treatment when he could quite easily have a masseuse at his beck and call at home. But not Tobias Moore. Every Friday, he lands his drone on the rooftop of the building which houses Sensual Healing, and makes his way down to our establishment on the 29th floor, flanked by his two bodyguards.

That first time when Loni summoned me, I'd been nervous as hell. If it wasn't enough that two beefy bodyguards had inspected my treatment room, then patted me down for weapons—as if I'd be carrying any—I then had to contend with Tobias Moore himself. Tall, powerful, charismatic, he'd appraised me with icy eyes. Why oh why had Loni picked me for this job? There were several master healers more experienced than me. But Loni had been insistent that I most closely fit the requirements of this client. And so there we were, alone in my treatment room once the bodyguards had retreated to stand outside. With shaking hands, I'd given him the tablet with a short questionnaire for him to complete and escorted him to the spa room. "I will leave you to soak in the spa bath as long as you wish," I'd murmured. "When you are ready, please come through to the next room and we shall begin the treatment."

He'd nodded brusquely, and I had left him to bathe in privacy. A minute later, my tablet had buzzed with the results of his questionnaire. I'd picked it up, curious to know what his treatment preferences were, and his limits. In short, he wanted the full range of treatments, including the prostate massage and penile stimulation. He did not like his ears to be touched. He did not wish to make any small talk. He would prefer to wear an eye mask for the entire treatment.

A few minutes later, he had walked into my treatment room, dressed in the robe I had left for him. He'd stopped at the massage bed, a look of enquiry on his face.

I'd handed him the eye mask he had requested and said, "If you will remove your robe and lie face down on the bed, we can begin."

Without a word, he had complied, untying the robe and throwing it carelessly on the chair. At the sight of his naked body, I had stifled a gasp. It's not every day that one is in close proximity with masculine perfection. My eyes drank in his broad, sculpted chest with everything in perfect proportion, and the magnificent dragon tattoo that spread its wings across his pecs—by the style of it, the work of the world-renowned artist, Levio. All too soon, he had turned, climbed onto the massage bed and placed the mask over his eyes before lying face down. Then, I had drizzled warm, aromatic oil onto his back and begun the massage.

I will never forget that first time I had the privilege to touch Tobias Moore. His tan skin was smooth and soft under the hardness of his musculature. His scent, subtle yet present under the aroma of the bath salts, was potently attractive. I couldn't put my finger on what it was exactly— something slightly woodsy with a strong dose of raw, unadulterated masculinity. Once I had started to stroke him, I had, curiously enough, lost all my nervousness. I fell into a hypnotic trance, not needing to instruct my hands in what to do. I just lost myself in the pure pleasure of touching him. There was no need to summon loving, joyful energy. It was there in abundance as I glided my palms along his skin, as I worshipped his glorious ass, as I kneaded his powerful thighs, and as I fisted his thick, long cock. When his cum had spurted out, I swear I'd felt an answering quiver in my pussy.

He had said nothing as I'd cleaned him up and covered him with a blanket. I'd left him to dress, walking past the burly bodyguards on my way out, conscious of the wetness in my panties. I had not expected him to return, but return he did, soon making it clear that he wanted me to be available for him every Friday at six pm. Without fail for the last two years, he has come for his treatment, tipping me generously each time. Not once has he cancelled. After a while, he dispensed with the eye mask, simply keeping his eyes closed as I massaged him. Soon too, the robe was discarded. After his bath, he towelled himself dry and strode out to my treatment room unabashedly naked. I could say that I have gotten used to the sight of his naked body, but that would be a lie. Each time, he takes my breath away.

Chapter 2

Tobias

It's Friday afternoon, and I've been plagued by restlessness the past few hours. There's no need to figure out why. I know it, clear as day. Friday is when I go see Viva. It's the one time in my week where I can relax totally. And yes, have a spectacular orgasm too. It is the one time in my schedule that is sacrosanct. No meeting, no business trip, nothing can interfere with my standing appointment at six pm. All my immediate staff are aware of this. They also see the effect it has on me, with my mood growing ever more surly as the week progresses, until Friday comes along and I get to have a reset.

At times, I've wondered whether I ought to schedule a second appointment with Viva during the week, but I've resisted the temptation. It's bad enough I'm addicted to my one fix of the week. Doubling that fix and that addiction is not a good idea.

Ever since my expensive divorce five years ago, I've been careful to keep women at bay. No girlfriend is going to worm her way into my life the way my ex did, only to try to sink her claws into my fortune with little regard for me or my feelings. It took a $6 billion settlement to get Serena out of my hair for good. Not ever going to do that again.

But much as it might shock some people, I am human and I do have physical needs. My solution has been to employ the services of a highly confidential and exclusive agency. Whenever I feel the need for sex, I summon an agency girl to my city penthouse—never to my house. We fuck, and then I send her away in my drone with little fuss and a fat tip to keep her happy. Though it's been a very long time since I've contacted the agency, come to think of it.

In addition to that, of course, I have my weekly appointment with Viva. I'd seen a media post about Sensual Healing and been attracted by the proposition. It seemed to fit with my need to have satisfying physical contact while keeping the whole thing business-like and transactional. I got my people to reach out to its owner, Loni Hughes, and she arranged a taster treatment with Viva. After that, it was a no-brainer for me. I made sure to clear my schedule every Friday for my session with her.

At precisely a quarter to six, I climb aboard the Tomo 3.1 drone, designed and fabricated by my own company, and program it to fly to my destination. Well actually, it's already programmed in. I simply activate it. Sven and Yuri flank me, as usual. I'm not exactly keen on having to be followed by bodyguards everywhere I go, but I've learned my lesson the hard way that they are, unfortunately, a necessity when someone has as much wealth as I do. They've been with me a few years now, and I'm used to them. They know to give me my space.

Soon, we're landing on the rooftop of the building where Viva works. The drone doors open and Sven jumps out, scanning the space before nodding for me to follow. We get into the elevator and take it down to the 29th floor. I enter the reception area of Sensual Healing, nodding a brisk greeting before striding down the long corridor to Viva's treatment room. By now, she will have been buzzed as to my arrival, for no sooner do I arrive at her door than it opens, and she greets me with a smile. "Good evening, Mr Moore," she says in a soft, melodious voice.

I stare into her face. She's beautiful. I didn't think it initially when I met her, but her beauty has grown on me. It's her brown eyes, large and soulful, that draw me in. That and her smooth golden skin. Too late, I realize I'm still standing at the threshold, staring into her eyes. "Viva, hello," I say brusquely.

I enter the room, leaving Sven and Yuri outside. After the first few times, it seemed pointless to have them search the room. As far as my physical safety is concerned, I trust Viva. Without another word, I follow her as she leads me to the spa room, with its tub filled with fragrant hot water. With a smile, she leaves me to undress and bathe. As she goes to shut the door behind her, I call out, "Leave it open." She hesitates, then nods and exits, leaving the door ajar. From where I am, I can see her move about the room, completing preparations for my treatment. Quickly, I undress and step into the spa bath, sighing in relief as my body is submerged in heat. I'm tempted to close my eyes, but I keep them open, looking out towards the treatment room. Viva is lighting some scented candles and placing them around the room. Then she's putting soft music on. I observe her face and supple body. As if she senses my gaze, she looks to me, then quickly looks away, not wanting to invade my privacy. I like that about her, the fact she respects my space. I cannot fault her professionalism—one more reason why I keep coming back.

I linger a minute or two more in the bath, letting its warmth seep into my body. Then I stand and step out, dripping water onto the mat. Viva's gaze is on me. Although I'm not looking her way, I can feel it. I look up to be sure. She turns away hastily, but not before I catch the flare of desire in her eyes. I've caught it once or twice before, and frankly, I'm glad I'm not the only one that feels this. Not that I plan to do anything about it, other than submit to her joyful ministrations on the massage bed. But undoubtedly, the desire I feel makes the massage a hundred times more pleasurable.

I reach out for a towel and dry myself, then prowl into the treatment room, my cock already semi-hard in anticipation of what is to come. Viva, still respecting my wish for no small talk, simply smiles and waits until I am settled face down on the large massage bed. There's a softly padded hole to place my nose and mouth through. I close my eyes and wait for that first magical touch of her hands on me. First, there's a drizzle of warm oil on my back. With gentle strokes, she disperses the oil all over my upper body. Then, she begins the massage. Placing two firm hands on either side of my spine, she glides them smoothly down to the small of my back, bringing them back up to start the downward glide again. I feel her bent over me as she strokes her hands down my body. She's so close I can breathe her scent in. I'm so familiar with it by now that I would sense her presence in any room, even blindfolded. It's a clean, fresh scent, with nothing artificial to it. It soothes me. I smile into the hole my face is in and settle down to enjoy my massage.

Taking her time, she kneads my neck and shoulders, ironing out the kinks, finding the right pressure points to sink her thumbs into and eliciting a moan from me. "That good?" she asks softly.

"Mmm," I grunt.

She continues, paying attention to every inch of my body. Her hands and forearms press into the cheeks of my ass. Fuck that feels good. The little tease grazes her fingers over my taint and just happens to flutter them over my ball sac. I know her game by now. She's edging me with her sensual routine, teasing me with little touches, making me crave more and more. It works. My cock is rock hard.

Finally, it's time to turn over. I settle down with my back on the firm mattress. Viva is careful to place a small pillow behind my head, so it's not wedged into that hole. Once she's ensured my comfort, she begins her massage again, drizzling more oil to my chest and abs. Her hands follow soon after, caressing, stroking, kneading. She plays with my nipples, circling them and rubbing them between her thumb and forefinger. I never thought much of that part of my anatomy before, but now? Fuck if it's not one of my most erogenous zones. There again, everywhere she touches feels incredibly good. Her hands glide down my arm, finding a pressure point along the inside of my elbow, then on my wrist. She takes my hand in hers and strokes deep circles into my palm. If I were a cat, I would be purring right about now. Each of my fingers get special attention, then it's time for my other arm to enjoy the same treatment. Every touch simultaneously calms and excites me. My cock is pointing straight up and dripping precum on my belly button. *For the love of God, woman, put your hands on it and bring me joy.*

But of course, she doesn't, not just yet. She shifts over to my legs, kneading the muscles of my thighs and teasing my groin with her touch on the upward stroke. I make a sound in the back of my throat which she has no trouble interpreting. "Soon," she promises, switching to my other leg and continuing with that exquisitely teasing massage along my thigh. And then, hallelujah, her hand is cupping my balls gently. I nearly rear off the bed. She places a firm hand on my thigh, holding me down. A moment later, I sense her reaching to the side table and pouring more oil into her hands. Then she's back, anointing my cock and balls with the oil, lubricating everything in readiness for what's to come. I open my eyes, taking in the alluring sight of her small hands on me.

She starts with slow, repetitive, rhythmic pulls of each hand along my shaft. She stares at it as if spellbound, attention concentrated on her task. Gradually, she increases the speed, jerking her hands up and down my cock, and fuck it feels good. She pauses momentarily to get more oil, this time massaging it over my asshole. She looks up at me then, a question in her eyes. "Yes," I grunt.

Permission granted, she eases a finger into my ass, probing gently until she finds my prostate. "There," I huff out. She presses into it intermittently and resumes her massage of my cock. There's surprising strength in her hand as she jerks my shaft while simultaneously milking my prostate. The pleasure is intense. I shut my eyes, unable to keep them open a moment more, and groan as I enjoy a long-drawn-out climax, spurting my cum into her hand. I lie back, spent, and feel her gently clean me up. Then a blanket is placed over me. I feel her press a palm over my heart, then she's bidding me farewell. "Thank you, Mr Moore. I hope to see you again next week. Peace be with you." And then she's gone, leaving me to rise at leisure and get dressed.

Chapter 3

Viva

I'm in the middle of Ms Rivera's treatment when we are interrupted by a knock on the door. I cover my client with a towel, excuse myself and go see what's up. It's very unusual to have this happen, so I know it must be something important. Outside my door, I see Loni, looking grim. I shut the door behind me to give us privacy. "What is it?" I ask, a feeling of dread creeping up on me.

"It's Joe. Your mom called. There's been an accident, some kid on a hoverbike knocked him down. They're on their way to Union Hospital right now. Go to your son, Viva; I'll take over here."

I'm frozen in shock. Ten thousand questions leap to my mind, chief of which is, "Is he okay?"

She purses her lips. "He's alive, but hurt. That's all I know. You need to go to him now. Take my drone from the rooftop. It'll be quicker."

I nod sluggishly. "Thanks," I murmur, then my feet are taking me to my locker in the staff quarters. Frantic now, I take my coat and bag, then run to the elevator. It's waiting for me, Loni already having thought to call it. I get in, press the rooftop button, and soon I'm whizzing up to the top of the building. I run to Loni's drone, pressing my palm to the panel for identification. A second later, there's a bleep and the drone door opens. "Union Hospital," I instruct it as I buckle my seatbelt on. In moments, the engine whirrs to life and I feel a whoosh as the drone is propelled upwards, before heading in the direction of the hospital.

I think to call Mom. She doesn't pick up, but a minute later, my communicator lights up with an incoming from her. She's in a white hospital corridor, walking hurriedly. "Viva, we just got here. The doctor's with Joe now, assessing his injuries."

"How bad is it, Mom?"

She shakes her head. "Honey, I don't know. It all happened so fast. We were at the road crossing when out of nowhere this hoverbike appeared and ran through the light. I tried to pull him back, but the bike clipped his side and somehow the strap of his backpack managed to get hooked into it." Her voice breaks as she continues, "He was dragged several yards before he fell to the road. He must have banged his head because he was unconscious when we got to him, and his arm was at an odd angle." She takes a calming breath in. "We'll know more once the doctor has seen him. How soon can you get here?"

I check the drone monitor screen. "I'm four minutes away."

"Good. I'll see you there."

"Yeah." We end the call, and I wait anxiously for the drone to arrive at the hospital, tapping my feet impatiently. I'm plagued by visions of my boy's small body being dragged along the road by a hoverbike. *Oh Lord, please let him be alright.*

As soon as the drone lands and its door has opened, I'm out, running to the hospital entrance. After a quick, breathless conversation with security, I'm directed towards the ER. Another run down a side corridor has me arriving in front of two large double doors with ER written above. I swing them open, looking around wildly for Mom. She waves at me from a small waiting area to my right. I hurry over to her. "Any news?" I ask.

"Nothing yet. Come sit with me, honey." She takes my arm and urges me to sit beside her. I collapse onto the worn, plastic chair, catching my breath. Mom takes my hand in hers. "Someone should come along soon to tell us what's happening. Stay positive."

I nod. "I'm trying."

We wait in tense silence, the minutes stretching out. A thought occurs to me. "Should I contact Dan?"

Mom's expression sours. "He's made it clear he wants nothing to do with his son. Now's not the time to open that can of worms."

"But if the worse happens—"

"We'll deal with it as it comes."

I feel my eyes well with hot, stinging tears. "I can't lose him, Mom."

"You won't. He's going to make it."

I wipe the tears with the back of my hand and sniff. I'm not a religious person, but I send a prayer to God that Mom's right. It's another six minutes before a green garbed medic approaches us. "Family of Joe Parker?" she asks.

"I'm his mom," I confirm. "How is he?"

She smiles reassuringly. "Ms Parker, I'm Dr Rosen. I'm hopeful your son will make a full recovery. He's had a concussion, so we'll need to keep him under observation for the next 24 hours. He also has a fractured arm which we've reset and put in a cast. There are some scratches and burns along the side of his face and arm, which we've cleaned and bandaged. Other than that, our scans show no internal injuries."

"Can I see him?"

"We'll be taking him up to the ICU shortly. I'll send a nurse to take you to see him just as soon as it's possible."

"Thanks, Dr Rosen," I say gratefully. "Is he conscious?"

"He regained consciousness, but we've sedated him for the pain. He's awake, just very drowsy."

"Okay."

She smiles, then leaves. Several minutes elapse before a nurse summons me to the ICU. Only one person can go in at a time, so Mom stays behind in the waiting area. My heart pounds in my chest as I approach Joe's bed. He looks so small and vulnerable, a large white cast on his arm and bandages along the side of his face. He's hooked to a machine that bleeps quietly beside him. I lower myself to the chair next to the bed and touch his hand gently. "Joe," I murmur. "It's Momma."

His eyes flutter, and he sees me. "Mom!" he cries plaintively. Then he begins to cry.

"Shh, it's gonna be alright. I'm here now, sweet boy."

"I was scared," he sobs.

"It's over now. You're safe." I stroke his hair back from his face and bend to kiss his forehead. "Try and get some sleep. Everything will feel better in the morning."

He settles down again and drifts off to sleep. I watch him, taking comfort in the rise and fall of his chest as he breathes. After a while, I go find Mom and let her have a turn watching over Joe. I find a bathroom, do my business and wash my face with cold water. My mind is beginning to function again after being in stasis this past hour. I start making plans. Mom and I will have to stay with Joe in shifts. I don't want him to wake up in a hospital bed alone. That means I'm going to need to take time off work. My finances will take a hit, but there's nothing I can do about it. I have some savings, which I'd put towards our next vacation. Worse come to the worse, I'll dip into those.

I call Loni and update her on Joe's condition. "I won't be in the rest of the week," I say.

"That's fine, Viva. Take all the time you need."

I bite my lip. "How about Mr Moore?" I ask, concerned.

"We'll let him know you've taken personal leave, and I'll have Suri take care of him next appointment."

"Sure," I say, but the thought of someone else giving him a treatment is oddly displeasing. I guess I've become so used to him being my client and not anyone else's. I can't help feeling some possessive jealousy. Foolish, I know. I force myself to focus on the matter at hand. "I don't know how long it will be before I'm back. Joe's going to need round-the-clock care until he's well enough to go to school again."

"As I said, take however much time you need," says Loni decisively.

"Thanks, Loni. I appreciate it."

"Send Joe my love and tell him to get well soon."

"I will." I end the call, feeling a renewed sense of purpose. Everything's going to be fine. We'll get through this just as we have every other challenge we've faced over the years. We're solid.

Chapter 4

Tobias

Thank fuck it's Friday. This has been the longest week. We've had protracted negotiations with SIPA, the Space and Inter-planetary Agency, which used to be known as NASA, over our proposal to enter into a partnership with the Venorians to build third generation spaceships. It's just under a year since we made first contact with this alien race, whose technology far exceeds our own. As soon as I heard about them, I knew that this was a golden opportunity for us to take a huge leap forward with our space technology. I've spent months cultivating my personal contacts with the Venorians, much to SIPA's displeasure. I've had talks with Krantor, one of the top figures in the Venorian government, and I believe they are a race we can do business with. But as usual, our own government lags behind, putting up obstacles in the name of security concerns, hence my meetings with their officials this week to try to get things moving. Come what may, I'm doing this deal.

I stretch my arms overhead. I'm done for today. I glance at the time. 17:37. Time enough to be heading over to Viva. I stand, addressing Ralph, my assistant. "I'm out of here. Don't contact me unless it's urgent."

"No problem," he responds.

I take the elevator to my rooftop, followed as ever by Sven and Yuri, who escort me to my drone. I activate it and we're off, flying into the dark November sky. Now that I'm on my way, I can't wait to get there. I close my eyes, conjuring Viva's beautiful face, her lovely smile with one dimple in the left cheek, the feel of her hands on me, her scent. Fuck how I need this. Not long to go.

We land and soon we're in the elevator making our way down to the 29th floor. We emerge into the reception area of Sensual Healing. I nod a brisk greeting and start striding down the corridor towards Viva's treatment room. "Mr Moore?"

Someone is hailing me. I turn around in annoyance. "What is it?" I grunt.

It's Loni, the owner of this place. She catches up with me and smiles ingratiatingly. "Mr Moore, I just wanted you to know that you'll be having Suri for your treatment today, as Viva has had to take some personal leave."

"Viva's not here?" I scowl.

"No, she's had to take personal leave. But I'm sure you'll love Suri. She's one of our best and most experienced master healers."

"But I want Viva."

"I'm afraid that won't be possible today," she says soothingly.

I stare at her, disappointment and frustration raging in my chest. Viva isn't here. I let out a breath. Okay then. Nothing to be done about it. Suri it is, whoever the hell she is. I turn abruptly and resume my walk to the treatment room. A slim, graceful looking young woman is there, smiling prettily. "Good evening, Mr Moore. Please do come in. I'm Suri, your master healer today."

I nod, but don't say anything. I let her lead me to the spa bath. She leaves, saying, "Please tap the button on the tablet if you need me, sir."

She closes the door behind her, and I set about meticulously undressing. I step into the bath and let the aromatic warmth of the water bubbling around me soothe my tired, aching body. Okay, so it's not Viva. It could still bring me some relief though.

I soak for a good ten minutes before I get out and dry myself. I slip on the robe and walk out of the bathroom. The room is set up as usual, the familiarity of it easing my mind. Quickly, I disrobe and climb onto the massage bed, lying face down. Suri is quiet, obviously having read my notes about not wanting small talk. Warm oil is drizzled on my back. With my eyes closed like this, I can almost believe it's Viva here with me.

Then two warm hands begin to stroke my back and I know that it's not Viva. It's pleasant enough, but she doesn't linger on that spot to the small of my back and release the tension there, like Viva does. She doesn't press on the point, just below my shoulder blades, which always brings me intense relief. Her kneading of my ass is a little too vigorous, lacking the sensual rhythm that Viva brings to it. Her light touch to my taint is unwelcome. I feel myself tighten, rather than loosen up.

I suffer through the rest of the massage, then turn to lie on my back. I'm not even sporting a semi. My cock has decided it's not interested in whatever Suri has to offer. As she leans over me to run her palms over my chest, I breathe in her scent. It's an earthy, musky aroma that unaccountably offends me. I feel my tension rising. She must sense this too, because she murmurs, "Relax. Let go."

In my experience, whenever anyone is told to relax, the opposite happens. I grit my teeth. She continues on with the treatment, mauling my arms and my legs. When I feel her hand cup my balls, I decide enough's enough. "Stop," I rasp.

She withdraws her hand instantly. "Of course, I'm sorry."

I sit myself up. "We're done here."

Her face falls. "Yes, sir. I do apologize if the treatment was not to your liking. Is there anything more I can do for you?"

"No, just leave me to get dressed."

She nods and walks out of the room, closing the door softly behind her. I get to my feet and quickly put on my clothes. Well, that was a fucking waste of time. Dressed, I leave the room, Sven and Yuri behind me as I stride down to the reception lobby. No surprise, Loni is there, preparing to do some damage limitation. I hold my hand up to pre-empt whatever it is she's going to say. "Save it, Loni. I'm sure Suri is a wonderful master healer, but she's not for me. I'll make sure she's paid for today and that she gets a good tip. However, let me be clear. It's Viva I want and no one else. Call me just as soon as she's back from her personal leave."

"Very well."

With that, I make my exit.

THE WEEKEND IS a washout, figuratively and literally. It rains nonstop, not helping my foul mood. Dad calls from whatever exotic island he's vacationing in with his latest nubile girlfriend who's half his age. I find dad irritating at the best of times, but for some reason, he's grating on me more so than usual. "All work and no play makes Tobias grumpy today," he chants in a singsong voice as he floats in the crystal clear water of the sea.

"Perhaps it's your smug tone that's making me grumpy, ever think of that?"

He pretends to look offended. "Smug, me? I just want to spread a little happiness to my ill-tempered son. Where's the harm in that?"

I sigh, pinching the bridge of my nose. "Apart from wanting to spread your special brand of happiness, was there any particular purpose to this call?"

"Just wanted to say hi. I'm thinking of you, son."

I try to smile, but it comes out more like a grimace. "I appreciate the thought, Dad."

"And I wanted to remind you that there's more to life than making billions—or is it trillions? Find yourself a nice girl and settle down."

An image of Viva flashes through my mind. I frown and chase the unwelcome thought away. "I'm doing just fine, Dad. Save yourself the concern."

"Not getting any younger, Tobias. About time you started a family and gave me another grandchild."

"Thirty-eight is hardly old," I say, feeling aggrieved, "and this kind of talk is so 21st century."

He shrugs. "I'm a product of the 21st century. Just think, Tobias. Before you know it, you'll be forty-eight and still with nothing to show for it except for a few trillion more dollars."

This conversation needs to stop, period. "Message received. Now if there's nothing else, I'll leave you to your frolic in the sea."

He smiles in amusement. "Peace out, son."

"Yeah, peace out," I grumble and end the call. My communicator bleeps, reminding me it's time for my daily workout. I change out of my clothes and head over to my personal gym. I've barely broken a sweat before there's another call, this time from Mom. What is it with the unwelcome calls today? I swear out loud, causing the virtual coach to ask in confusion, "Is there a problem, sir?"

"Pause program," I reply in frustration and snatch up my communicator.

Mom appears on the screen, "Darling, have I caught you at a bad time?"

"Hey Mom, I'm in the middle of a workout."

She raises a brow. "I see that. Well, I won't keep you. I just wanted to confirm you're coming for Thanksgiving."

It's next Saturday. If the date had fallen on a Friday, it would have been a "no" from me. But as it is, with Viva surely back next week, I plan to fly out to Mom's estate in Maine the morning after my treatment session at Sensual Healing. I hope it will put me in a reasonably cheerful frame of mind, which will help to withstand the rigors of a family get together. The Moores are not what I would call a happy, cosy family. On two holidays of the year, Thanksgiving and Christmas, we make a show of unity. Dad attends the gatherings, sans girlfriend, and likewise, Mom's long-term companion, Miguel, makes a tactful exit, electing to spend the holiday with his own family in California. That leaves us only with my older sister, Mia, her Scottish fiancé, Rory, whom she plans to wed in some castle in the Highlands next year, and Noah, her teenage son from a previous relationship. If I'm honest, Noah is probably the only one that I look forward to seeing.

"I'll be there," I say in reply.

"Good. I suppose it's too much to expect you'll be bringing a female friend with you?"

What is it with this subject today? "Just me," I say shortly. "Now if you don't mind, Mom, I need to get back to my workout."

"Not at all. Go in peace, Tobias."

"Yeah, you too."

Somehow, I get through the weekend and the following few days, though I am perhaps a touch more irritable. My staff know me well enough to give me space when I'm like this. Still, I can't imagine I'm pleasant to be around. All because one fucking person decided to go on personal leave. It can't be right that my own wellbeing hinges on that one person. Just as soon as she's back, and I'm on an even keel again, I'm going to have to deal with this issue. Either ensure permanent access to Viva or find myself a suitable back-up. Maybe I need to try out the rest of the master healers and see if there is someone else that suits me. Perhaps the disastrous session with Suri was a fluke.

Ralph pages me on my communicator. "What is it?" I bark.

He ignores my scowl and says, "I think you'll be interested in this latest piece of news. I've just heard from a source that the State Department will soon be announcing a cultural exchange program with the Venorians. The plan is to send five humans to live on the planet Ven for six months and to have five Venorians come and live here in the US in their place. The announcement will be going out next Tuesday, and they'll be inviting candidates to apply soon after. They'll be the first humans to set foot on that planet. I thought perhaps we might want one of our people on that exchange."

"You thought right. There is one person I can think of who would be perfect for the job."

"Troy Summers?"

"You read my mind. Can you send him over here?"

Ralph smirks. "Already have. He's outside your door. Shall I let him in?"

"Do that, and come sit in on the meeting."

A moment later, my office door slides open and Troy walks in, followed by Ralph. I direct them to my thinking nook—it's a circular space with spectacular views over to the Hudson bay. Four malleable armchairs that can rotate 360 degrees are scattered around the space. They're made to my specifications, temperature controlled and designed to mould around the body to provide gravity-defying support. I pad over to one of them in my bare feet. I rarely wear shoes when I'm in the office. Why should I? I settle myself in one of the armchairs and place my feet on the automatic massager, programming it at medium intensity. My other two guests follow suit.

Once we're comfortable, I get to the point of this meeting. "Troy, good to see you. If you'll pardon the question, are you still single and unattached?"

He puts a hand to his heart. "Tobias, if this is your unsubtle way of asking me out, then the answer is a resounding yes."

I snort. "Sorry to disappoint. Still not into guys. I'm asking for a different reason."

He mock sighs. "One lives in hope. So, what's up?"

"You interested in going to live on the planet Ven for six months?"

He sits up, narrowing his eyes. "Tell me more."

I let Ralph do the explanations, then add my own thoughts, "With your background in space engineering and your photographic memory, I'm certain you'd be able to collect invaluable data for our spaceship project. This is a one-of-a-kind opportunity to explore a highly evolved alien society and learn whatever you can from them. What do you say?"

"I say, sign me up," Troy grins.

Ralph, ever the practical person, feels duty bound to interject, "Of course, you'll have to put forward your candidacy and go through the selection process like everyone else."

I wave my hand. "He'll get selected. Everyone on the selection panel will know Troy works for me, and trust me, no one wants to get on my bad side." It's true. I don't even have to bribe anyone. Just the specter of offending me is enough to sway decisions my way. I'm not unaware of the power I hold.

We talk logistics a bit more, then I end the meeting, feeling more upbeat than I have in days. All the pieces are beginning to come together for my spaceship project with the Venorians. Whenever I'm on the cusp of a major deal, I get a tingle in my bones. I'm feeling it now. This is going to put all my previous projects in the shade. I go home later that day feeling mostly human, not the disgruntled dinosaur of before. Plus, tomorrow, it's Friday.

Chapter 5

Viva

I'm back at Sensual Healing this evening for one reason only: Tobias Moore. I would have preferred to finish the week out at home with Joe, celebrate Thanksgiving and then return to work the following week, but Loni contacted me, a touch of panic in her voice, asking if I could make it back just for this one client. Apparently, things did not go well with Suri last week. Am I gloating? Maybe a little.

Mom has agreed to hold the fort with Joe while I'm out. He's mostly recovered from his accident. The grazes and burns on his face have healed remarkably quickly, with only a faint pink scarring to be seen, and even that should fade eventually too. His arm is still in a cast, of course, but I've spoken to his school and they'll provide him with the additional support he needs. Tuesday after Thanksgiving, he'll be back in class.

I walk into the reception lobby at Sensual Healing and on hearing my voice, Loni comes out from her office to greet me with a massive hug. "Viva, good to see you. How's Joe?"

"He's doing well. Getting a little bit antsy at home. I sure will be glad when he's back in school."

"And we sure are glad to have you back here. Mr Moore's assistant called this morning to ask if you'd be in today. That man needs your services urgently."

I smile. "He'll get all the attention he needs, I promise."

"Good. I can tell you, I do not want to get into his bad books."

"I'll do all I can to get things back on track," I reiterate.

She nods, satisfied. "You go now and get yourself set up."

Dismissed, I head over to my treatment room and start getting it ready, setting things up just the way Mr Moore likes. At five to six, I start filling up the spa bath. For some reason, my pulse is racing with a combination of excitement and nerves. It's almost like the first time he came for a treatment. It's silly, I know. He's been coming here for years, and this should go like clockwork. But nothing is ever routine where Tobias Moore is concerned. Here, in the privacy of the spa room, I can admit to myself that I've missed him, more than a little. Yeah, a client who barely says two words to me, for whom I'm probably just a convenient vessel for his physical release. I mean, if that's not scratching the barrel of desperation, I don't know what is.

What I need, is to get laid. When was the last time I had sex with a human, not a vibrating toy? Too long. And sadly, I know the reason why. Ever since I laid my hands on the perfection that is Tobias Moore, no man has stood the comparison. Truth time now. That too long since I've had sex? More like two years. I need to get a fucking life.

Loni's voice interrupts my thoughts, warning me through the speakers, "He's on his way."

I straighten up, giving myself a quick glance in the mirror. Everything is neatly in place, looking professional. I take a deep breath and go open the door. Tobias Moore is there, flanked by his two bodyguards. I paste a nervous smile. "Good evening, Mr Moore." He glowers at me. Without a word, he strides past me to the spa room. I shut the door gently, catching the curious eyes of one of the bodyguards. He shrugs, as if to say, "Good luck." Looks like I'll be needing it.

I hover in the treatment room, waiting for Tobias to emerge from his bath. He's left the door ajar and I can see him unbuttoning his shirt. I turn away and start lighting some scented candles. "Viva!" His voice is like whiplash. "Come here."

I set down the candle and walk hesitantly to the spa room. His shirt is off, and he's busy undoing his pants. "Where the fuck have you been?" he demands.

His pants are off now, and so are his boxer briefs. I'm bereft of speech.

"Answer me! What the fuck was so important that you had to cancel on me last week?" This is more words than he's uttered to me in a whole two years. He stands with his hands on his hips, unconcerned with his nakedness.

"I-I had to take personal leave."

He huffs, his nostrils flaring. "What kind of lame-assed excuse is that?" Abruptly, he turns and steps into the bath, lowering himself to a sitting position and hissing as he's engulfed in heat. But he's not done. He reclines on the bath pillow and glares, ripping into me again, "You have all the time from Saturday to Thursday to take leave, but every Friday, without fail, you are required here. Look at me, Viva."

I look up from the floor I've been scrutinising with unwarranted interest. The harangue then continues. "I lead a trillion dollar conglomerate," he grits, "employ eight hundred and sixty seven thousand people and have thousands clamoring for my time each day, but do you see me miss any of our appointments? Have I ever even been late coming here? Have I?" His voice has risen to a roar.

"No," I mutter.

"That's right. I am always right on time, every Friday at six pm. So why the fuck can't you be there too? Do you know, Viva, how your absence last week impacted my wellbeing? How it reduced my ability to concentrate? If I were to crunch the numbers, why I'd bet you were responsible for the loss of millions of dollars. What do you have to say about that?"

What do I have to say? My nerves have morphed into blazing anger. I let loose. "It could be billions of dollars for all I care. You want to know why I missed our appointment last Friday? Well, I'll tell you. My son, my sweet six-year-old boy, was knocked over by a hoodlum on a hoverbike and rushed to hospital unconscious. I'm sorry, Mr Moore, if that impacted your wellbeing and your ability to make millions, but none of that is as important to me as the welfare of my son."

I pivot and walk out of the spa room, shutting the door behind me. Now that the words are out, I'm smitten by worry and regret. What was I thinking, shouting at my most lucrative client? I should have bitten my tongue and swallowed my pride. With shaking hands, I busy myself lighting more candles and selecting ambient music to play. It's another five minutes before the door opens and Tobias Moore comes in, naked, drops of water still trickling down his chest from where he's impatiently towelled himself dry. He goes to the massage bed and sits on the edge, but doesn't lie down.

"Your son. What's his name?" he asks.

"His name is Joe."

His eyes burrow into me. "How's Joe doing now?"

"He's doing ok. He still has a cast on his arm, but apart from that, the rest of his injuries have healed."

He nods. "That's good. Who's with him now? His dad?"

I give a short laugh. "No, the man who spawned him is long gone. He's with my mom, and after Thanksgiving, he'll be back at school."

Tobias continues to watch me intently. In a low voice, he says, "Viva, come here."

I approach him cautiously until I'm standing directly opposite him, a few feet away. He reaches out to pull me closer until my clothed legs knock against his bare ones. "I'm sorry," he declares, his gray eyes laser focused on mine. "I should not have said the things I did."

"No," I agree. Then I add for good measure, "Apology accepted."

He nods briskly, letting me go, and turns to settle himself face down on the bed. Alrighty then. Now that's out of the way, let's get down to business. I take the bottle of oil that's been warming on the hot plate and drizzle some on his back. Then my hands begin to stroke his smooth skin, caressing the planes of his muscular frame. I lose myself in the joy of touching him again. I lean down, perhaps a little closer than I should, and breathe him in, inhaling his heady scent. My hands glide down to his firm buttocks. A work of art, I think, as I press my palms there in a circular motion. I find the point on the small of his back and pulse down on it, releasing the tension that's built up there. He groans, "Fuck yes."

I drizzle more oil. With my hands flat, I make a circular tour of his buttocks, pressing down to the top of his thighs then coming back around and starting all over again. Round and round I go, parting his cheeks on the descent and lightly grazing his taut testicles. He's fully aroused. I continue my massage, paying attention to the back of his thighs, his calves, his feet. Every inch of him is perfection, every touch of his skin a silken pleasure. I pause at his feet and say softly, "In your own time, please turn around and lie on your back."

He swivels his body around, his eyes searching mine. My breaths are sharp and shallow. His cock is thickly engorged. Quickly, I get a small pillow to put under his head. He stops me with a hand on my arm as I'm about to get the oil. "Put your hands on me, Viva," he whispers huskily. "I can't wait a minute more." His meaning is clear.

I nod, grabbing the oil and pouring some into my palm. Then I'm stroking my oiled hands over his swollen shaft and balls. At my touch, he makes a needy moan. I fist his cock with both hands and begin to stroke my way from root to tip, running my thumb over his slit, which is oozing precum. He's so turned on, I don't think I'll be needing to stimulate his prostate. His eyes never leave me as I caress him, my hands fisting him strongly, pulsing up and down in a rapid motion. He groans, "Yeah. Oh yeah." His cock swells impossibly more. I know he's close. And then I do the opposite of what protocol dictates. I lean closer as I jerk him, wanting to see, wanting...

With a rough cry, he spurts his release, some of it catching on my hand but a thick stream landing on my chin, just below my lips. Reflexively, I lick it into my mouth, his flavor exploding on my tongue. His eyes flare as he holds my stare. In a rush, common sense floods back, and I step away quickly, going to wash my hands and wipe off the rest of his cum from my chin. Then I grab a wet cloth and go to clean him up. He says nothing, but follows my every movement with his eyes. Once I'm done, I say a little shakily, "I will massage your front now." He nods slightly, closing his eyes. I drizzle oil on his chest and begin.

His eyes remain closed as I stroke his chest, his arms, his thighs. His breathing is deep and relaxed, so deep in fact that I suspect he's fallen into a light doze. When I'm done, I cover him with a blanket and press two hands to his chest. "Mr Moore, thank you again for your patronage. Take all the time you need to get dressed. I look forward to seeing you again next week."

His hands traps mine to his chest. "Viva." His eyes are wide open now, gazing at me. "That was good. Thank you."

"You're welcome," I murmur.

Still, he holds my hands. "You doing anything special for Thanksgiving?"

"Nah. It'll just be me, Joe, my mom and Trey. He's kind of her boyfriend, though she won't admit it. They started seeing each other a few years after my dad passed."

"Sounds like it'll be more fun than my obligatory family reunion," he says softly.

"Not close to your family?"

He snorts. "Let's just say we're better off keeping our distance."

"Oh." I bite my lip, not knowing what to say.

"Mom and Dad are separated," he explains, "but for some obscure reason feel the need to put on a united front at the holidays."

"Ouch. That sounds painful."

He smiles. "It is. The only bright spot on the horizon is my nephew, Noah. He's fifteen and hasn't had a chance yet to become jaded like the rest of us."

"Well, that's something to look forward to, catching up with him."

"Yeah. I guess so." He's silent, still trapping my hands to his chest. "I'll see you next week?"

"I promise." Then I add, "Unless there's some kind of emergency."

"There better not be," he grunts. "Happy Thanksgiving, Viva."

"Happy Thanksgiving." He releases my hands finally, and I head out the door.

Later, as I'm making my way home on the super-subway, my communicator buzzes with a notification. I've been paid both for today and last week's missed appointment, with a generous tip. I put the communicator away, a faint smile forming on my face. Under that brusque exterior, I do believe there beats a warm and kind heart in Tobias Moore.

Chapter 6

Tobias

Thanksgiving was not as excruciating as I expected it to be. Unusually, Mom and Dad seemed positively cordial with one another, each having reached a happy state of existence in their own lives, enough to want to bestow positivity to those around them. Mia did not annoy me like she always does, and her fiancé, Rory, failed to bore me with drunken tales of his Highland ancestors.

Perhaps the reason why my family was surprisingly tolerable had nothing to do with them and everything to do with me. Ever since my session with Viva last Friday, I've been in remarkably good humor. One scene replays over and over in my mind. That of Viva licking my cum from her face. It awakens a primal, possessive part of me that has lain dormant for years, decades even. I want her.

Something between us shifted last Friday. I'm sure that Viva will put on a professional front when I next visit her and pretend that all is the same as usual. But I know, and she knows, that's not true. The question is, what to do about it.

I had promised myself that I would deal with the issue just as soon as I was back on an even keel, that I would find a way to either ensure permanent access to Viva or a suitable back-up. Well, the back-up idea is a bust. It's Viva I want. And I want her for more than just sensual massages.

I don't date or do girlfriends though. I'm not ready to open myself up to that kind of thing again. Besides, she's got a child, which complicates matters. I'm a high profile person, much as I dislike it, and I'm not going to inflict on her or her son the level of public scrutiny that would come with dating me.

I could go the transactional route, which is usually my preferred option—private and intimate access to her in return for a generous payment. There's nothing wrong with sex work. It's a legal profession which fulfils a vital human need for physical connection. However, I sense that Viva would not be agreeable to such terms. She's always keen to maintain the utmost professionalism in her dealings with me, except for that last time of course. What she does at Sensual Healing could already by some people's standards be classified as sex work, but I know Viva doesn't see it that way and that she wouldn't want to go down that path any further. So, whatever arrangement we end up having cannot involve the payment of money.

I suppose the answer is to have a friends-with-benefits type of arrangement, to coin an archaic 21st century phrase. More like an acquaintance-with-benefits kind of thing. We're hardly what one would call friends. The more I think of it, the more I warm to the idea. I could have her come to my penthouse once or twice a week for a mutually satisfying, uncomplicated good time. All very discreet, so no one apart from ourselves and my closest entourage would need to know. That could work. I'll have to finetune my pitch between now and next Friday, make sure I put it to her in a way that will get her to say yes. I can do that.

Now that the decision is made, I chafe at the days still left until Friday. My mood, unfortunately, goes downhill as I battle my frustration. She had better the hell say yes to my plan.

Chapter 7

Viva

Joe's back at school, and I'm back to my normal working routine. Except nothing's quite the same as before. Clients come in and out of my treatment room, and I try to give them the utmost blissful experience as I always do. But my mind, which should be focused on them, is somewhere else.

It keeps going back to that moment with Tobias Moore when my veneer of professionalism was shattered and splintered into a million tiny pieces. I've been doing this job for three years, and never have I crossed that line before. My work involves intimate touch and sexual stimulation, yet it has always adhered to a strict protocol, one that I failed to follow when I leaned close and took Tobias's cum on my face. I could have brushed it off as an accident, but not what I did afterwards. I licked his cum like a cat that got the cream. Damnit!

He had seen me do it too. The look he'd given me had been unmistakably feral, like a lion that had spotted its prey. In that moment, I knew. Tobias Moore wants me, maybe almost as much as I want him. Such a realization is not an easy one to come back from. Hence my preoccupation.

What to do about it? What can I possibly do? He's my most valuable client, and I can't afford to lose him. Mustn't rock the boat. The only thing I can do is go back to business as usual where he's concerned. Be disciplined. Keep a tight rein on my desires.

That's what I say to myself at just a few minutes to six on Friday. I check my appearance in the mirror to ensure I look as neat and professional as possible. Deep breath in, deep breath out. Just going to treat this as a routine appointment.

"He's here," a voice alerts me from the reception lobby.

I walk to the door and open it. Tobias stands before me, dominating the space. His presence hits me like a sucker punch. Routine appointment my ass. I can't stop my heart pounding in my chest and my whole body pulsing with energy. That's the effect this man has on me. With an effort, I smile, "Good evening, Mr Moore."

"Hello, Viva," he responds, the deep timbre of his voice reverberating through every cell in my body.

He strolls inside and makes his way towards the spa room. I remain where I am, giving him space. From the corner of my eye, I see him undress and enter the steaming bath.

"Viva, come here!" he barks.

My feet take me to the doorway. He waves me in impatiently. "Keep me company while I bathe," he says, in a departure from his usual pattern. He nods towards the plush chair beside the tub.

Hesitantly, I settle onto the edge of it, keeping my back ramrod straight. He observes this with an amused quirk to his lips. "How are you, Viva?" he asks, as if it's totally natural for him to engage in such small talk.

"I'm well, thank you. And you?"

"Just peachy."

I look down at my hands, clutched in my lap. Well, this is awkward. He observes me as a silence falls between us. Then, "Viva, I've been thinking."

I look up. "Yes?"

"I'm not one to beat about the bush, so I'm just going to say it. Viva, I want you."

I nod, as if that makes perfect sense. "You want me," I repeat like an idiot.

His eyes drill into me. "That's right."

"What exactly do you mean by that?" I venture to ask.

He continues to fix me with his stare. "It means, Viva, I want you to talk to at the end of a long day, and to share a meal with. It means I want you in my bed. It means I want you to be mine and mine alone. Now look me in the eye and tell you don't want that too."

I dodge the question with another. "You're asking me to date you?"

"No, I don't date, at least not in public. I do, however, want to spend time with you, and I think you want it too."

That clears things up. Not really. "So," I try to clarify, "we'd see each other casually in private, and be exclusive for however this thing lasts?"

He leans forward suddenly, his elbow on the edge of the tub. "Nothing about us is casual, Viva. But yes, I want to spend time with you, alone and far from prying eyes. And yes, it would be exclusive."

"I don't have that much time to spare for alone time with you," I say consideringly. "You know I have a son."

"I know you have a son. I won't take your whole time with him, only I think you could spare one evening a week to be with me. Can we agree to that? Surely your mom or someone you trust can look after him during that time?"

"Possibly. I'd have to ask her."

"So, is that a yes?"

I try to think objectively. Could I do this? "What about your treatments here at Sensual Healing? Would they stop?"

"Hell no! That stays as it is, Fridays at six. But I'd want to see you in addition to that."

"Could we keep things professional here, once we cross that line?" I worry my lip.

He stands and steps out of the bath. I watch him as he towels himself dry, but still he doesn't answer. He drops the towel and holds out his hands to me. Without thinking, I take them, and he pulls me from the chair on which I've been perched. Very slowly, giving me ample time to back out, he brings his lips to mine. We stand facing each other, hands clasped together. His kiss is gentle, exploratory, almost tender. It's that gentleness that undoes me. Up till now, I've felt like a coiled spring that's been ready to let loose, but at his tender touch, something eases deep inside of me. I close my eyes, letting the warmth of his hands on mine and the softness of his kiss soothe my soul. My pounding heart returns to its normal beat.

Just as gently, he ends the kiss, pulling back to look at me but still holding on to my hands. Softly, he says, "This is your place of work, Viva, and I respect that. When I'm here, it's as your client. I can stick to the rules if you can." He grins wickedly. "But no more licking of my cum, dirty girl, or else I can't answer for what I will do."

I don't know if it's his reminder of that professional lapse or his calling me dirty girl that brings a flush to my face. "I won't do that again," I breathe.

"Oh, you will, but not here," he says, full of confidence.

"I haven't agreed to this yet," I remind him.

"Then think about it while you give me my massage, and tell me your decision afterward." He lets go of my hand and nods towards the treatment room.

"Okay," I say.

I lead him out of the spa room and wait for him to get settled on the massage bed. Then, I begin the treatment. As I run my oiled hands over his body, I think through his offer. Being his secret lover is not exactly the height of my romantic dreams. Let's face it though. A romance with the likes of Tobias Moore has never been on the cards. And ever since my rat of an ex ran out on me after I got pregnant, romance has not been high on my list of priorities. This is more like a pragmatic arrangement where we each get something out of it without otherwise disrupting the day-to-day rhythm of our lives. What is there to lose?

I come to the end of the treatment and place the blanket over Tobias. I press my hands to his chest and say, in my most professional tone, "Thank you for your patronage today, Mr Moore. In your own time, please sit yourself up and make sure you rehydrate."

His hands trap mine as I'm about to step away. Eyelids flutter open as he brings his gaze to me. "Your answer, Viva," he commands.

I take a deep breath. "Yes," I say in response.

He smiles in satisfaction. "Good. I've made my communicator accessible to yours. Just say my name into your apparatus and it will connect with mine instantly. Call me anytime, Viva, and I mean anytime. Let me know what evening works for you."

"Okay," I murmur.

He releases my hands. I head towards the door, then pause and look his way. "Bye," I mumble shyly.

"Bye, Viva. Until next week."

Chapter 8

Viva

I take the super-subway and head over to Mom's place. She's in the kitchen with Joe when I arrive, and they're busy making cookies. "Hey Mom," I say in greeting, then swoop my arms around my boy, rubbing my cheek to his. "What is that you're making?" I ask, pretending ignorance.

He laughs excitedly. "It's chocolate chip cookies, my favorite!"

"And mine too."

"Here, let me take these," says Mom, taking the tray and sliding it into the oven. She scrutinizes me. "You hungry?"

"Starving. What's for dinner?"

"Pasta and meatballs," answers Mom. Plant-based of course. Unless you're super rich like Tobias Moore, real meat is a rare luxury saved for special occasions. I don't mind. I've grown to like the micro-protein mince almost as much as the real thing. I can't help but wonder though, what kind of food will be on offer during my weekly dates with Tobias. I suspect it will be a step up from what I'm accustomed to, no doubt prepared by his own chef. Is it wrong of me to feel a thrill at the prospect? I'm going to be secretly dating the richest man in the world.

What must it be like to be him? I've always thought it insane, bordering on the obscene, for one person alone to be so rich. That's not to mean that Tobias hoards his money. Over the years, I've given in to my curiosity and read up all I could find about him. I've learned that he has set up multiple charitable foundations, that he personally sponsors the education and housing of hundreds of people he takes an interest in, and that he's single-handedly responsible for the building of the hyperloop network across the African continent, kickstarting a transport and communications revolution that has seen per capita GDP rise by twenty per cent in just five years.

However, he seems to generate money just as fast as he spends it, having a canny knack for investing in obscure startups that end up being major successes. The man is a genius on another level, added to which he's beautiful and sexy. Could life get any more unfair? And he wants me. I can't stop my face from beaming.

Mom looks at me suspiciously. "What was that grin all about?" she demands.

"I love pasta and meatballs," I say innocently.

"Don't try to pull one on me. Something's happened."

I relent. "Perhaps." Glancing at Joe, I add, "Can't talk now."

"Okay then, let's eat."

I help set the table—Mom has never believed in the need for a house bot—and we sit down to eat. After dinner, I settle Joe down in his virtual play space where he can experience fun stories and interact with his favorite characters, all in a safe, child appropriate way. Once we have privacy, Mom and I sink into the two malleable armchairs in her living room—sold by one of Tobias's many companies—and place our feet in the massage nook. I sigh happily as I feel the artificial hands press the acupressure points on my tired feet. I've always maintained that human touch is a thousand times superior to artificial massagers, but I'll admit there is a time and a place for such things.

For a while, we're both quiet as we relax and let our bodies recharge. Finally, Mom speaks. "So, are you going to tell me?"

"It's Tobias Moore," I say.

She huffs. "What has your favorite trillionaire done now?"

I'm not sure how to tell her about the arrangement he has proposed. I settle for, "He wants to date me, but in private, without the world knowing."

"And how's that going to work?"

"He suggested I spend time with him at his place, if you could take care of Joe one evening a week."

She doesn't respond straight away. I look across at her and find her frowning. Finally, she says, "You're an adult, Viva, and it's not my place to tell you how to live your life. I'm always happy to have Joe, so that's not a problem."

Not a raving endorsement, but there again, I never expected one. "You think I'm making a mistake?"

She shakes her head. "No, it's not that. I'm not even surprised by this. The way you've talked about him over the years, it was clear that something was up between the two of you. Just, be careful."

"I will be."

"Okay then."

We don't talk any more about it. Ten minutes later, I leave Mom's house with Joe. Luckily, my place is just a short walk down the block. It's late, so I start his bath then ready him for bed. In his room, I let him choose a book and sit with him on the big armchair to read. I hold his little body to mine, my hand touching the cast on his arm. In another two weeks, it should hopefully come off.

We get to the end of the book and I see him stifle a yawn. "Time for bed," I tell him.

"Can we read another story, please Momma?"

"You're tired, sweet boy, and you have school tomorrow."

He pouts. "I'm not tired. I want another story." I know he gets cranky the more tired he is and that he's gearing himself up for a meltdown. Experience has taught me that saying no point blank will get me nothing but trouble, though I don't like to give in to his demands. A suitable compromise is what's required here.

"How about this," I say. "You get into bed, and I'll dim the light. If you're still awake after five minutes, then I'll read you another story. Now I have to get myself out of these day clothes. I'll come back as soon as I'm done. Deal?"

He considers the matter, then nods. I lower him off my lap and go put the book back on the shelf while he obediently gets into bed, saying, "I want the story about the velociraptor."

"Ask nicely, Joe. Say 'please may I have the story about the velociraptor' next time. If you're still awake when I get back, I'll read it to you."

"I will be," he says confidently.

I kiss his soft cheek. "We'll see. I love you, Joe."

"Love you too."

I dim the light and leave the room with the door ajar, telling him, "I'll be back in five." In actual fact, it'll be more like ten minutes, just to make sure he has time to fall asleep, but I don't tell him that. One of a mother's little white lies.

In my room, I shed my clothes, pull on a comfy house bra, my pastel blue nightshirt and fluffy socks. I brush my teeth and wash my face, then rub moisturizer into my skin. It's chilly, so I add a woolly cardigan to my house ensemble. Then, very quietly, I tiptoe to Joe's room. As expected, he's fast asleep. I tuck the blanket around him more securely and carefully exit the room again.

It's nearly nine pm. I make my way to the living room, communicator in hand, and settle on my malleable armchair. I could watch the latest instalment of the drama series I've been following or I could read. I'm currently halfway through a historical romance set in the 1980s during the cold war era, about a Russian ballerina who falls in love with an American hockey player while on tour in the States. Neither option seems appealing just now.

I blow out a breath. When had my life gotten quite so lonely? Granted, I've never been the most gregarious of people, but I used to hang out with friends, eating out or seeing live bands. I used to date random men on my favorite dating app, the dates occasionally turning into something a little more long-term. The last one such was Joe's father, who I dated for five months before accidentally getting pregnant. It's pretty hard to become accidentally pregnant in this day and age, what with contraception being as medically advanced as it is. The fact that it happened seemed like a sign to me, an act of god telling me Joe was meant to be. For Dan, it was a betrayal. He claimed I must have somehow done it on purpose to trap him, catch that he is. I've never had a man run out on me faster than he did that day, never to be heard from again except for the documents sent through his lawyers, waiving his parental rights. I could have fought them in the courts, but I didn't. If he didn't want to be part of Joe's life, then we were better off without him.

Since then, my son has been my prime focus. I enrolled at the elite Sensual Healing program, working hard to gain my certification so that I could earn enough to give him a good roof over his head, send him to a decent school, and afford to buy him the material things he deserves. We've done alright, but my social life suffered in the collateral damage. Evenings out became evenings in. Whenever I've felt the need for sex, I've scratched that itch with upgraded sex toys, or very occasionally, with dates on my app. I still meet up with friends when I can spare the time, though it hasn't helped that Evie, my bestie, moved across the ocean to live in Paris three years ago.

And so here I am, aged twenty-nine, alone on a Friday evening. Is Tobias lonely too, I wonder? It can't be easy being the richest man in the world. Is that why he comes to see me at Sensual Healing? I've been curious about why a man who seems to have everything, feels the need to pay a stranger to touch him intimately once every week. Although, come to think of it, we're no longer strangers. Somehow, without words but through touch, we've built a rapport over the years. I feel like I know him—perhaps not the ins and outs of his life, but the essence of who he is. It's like I can sense it through the exchange of energy that occurs during treatments. I guess that's an esoteric way to think about our relationship. All I know is that there is an answering need in me to be with him. I pick up my communicator.

"Athena," I instruct the computer interface, "call Tobias Moore."

In seconds, he answers the call, staring at me with his penetrating gray eyes. "Viva," he says in that deep voice. "It's good to hear from you." He's dressed casually in a sweatshirt and seems to be reclining on a malleable chair much like mine—well, he's made billions from designing and manufacturing them. "Joe gone to sleep?"

I smile. "Like a light."

"That's good. Is he an easy-going child?"

"Yeah, he is. I mean there are the occasional tantrums, but for the most part he's chill."

"Like his mom," says Tobias.

"You think? I can get pretty worked up."

His eyes gleam. "That, I'd like to see."

I laugh. "Stick around, Tobias, and you will."

He cuts to the chase. "When can I see you, Viva?"

"You free on Tuesday?"

"I'll make myself free. What time do you finish at Sensual Healing? I'll send my drone to pick you up."

My lips quirk into an amused smile. "What, you're not going to let me go home first and prettify myself?"

He leans forward in his chair, as if he wants to get closer to me. "Look at you, Viva," he says in a deep, throaty voice, "dressed down and scrubbed clean of make-up, and I can't think of anything prettier."

I feel my cheeks redden. I know I'm decent looking, and I'm hardly lacking in body confidence, but the look on his face as he said this has me getting all worked up. "Right," I mutter. "I'm done at six fifteen."

"Then I'll expect you here by six thirty."

"Okay."

He sits back and asks idly, "What are you doing the rest of this evening?"

"I was debating between watching something or reading," I say on a sigh. "You?"

"Same. You want to watch something with me? I have the latest pre-release from Barton Muir."

"You do? Why am I surprised, of course you would." Barton Muir is the biggest name in immersive films, directing and starring in a host of acclaimed action dramas. I think I've immersed myself in his last movie, Clench, at least half a dozen times.

Tobias raises a brow. "You in or not?"

"I'm in," I hurry to say.

"Okay, I'll patch you in to my feed. Where would you like to be? Center or on the edge?"

Center is like being dropped into the skin of the main protagonist in any scene, seeing the events unfold from their perspective. On the edge means being an observer of all the characters while still being immersed in the action.

I like to think of it as the movie equivalent of first person or third person narrative in a book. "I don't mind," I say truthfully. "I always end up watching his movies more than once and changing perspective. What do you prefer?"

"I like to be the third eye and live on the edge," he deadpans.

"Well, then let's do it."

In moments, he's patched me in. I turn off all the lights, putting my living room in pitch darkness. The door's closed, shutting out any loud sounds that might disturb Joe, though I have a monitor in his room that will alert me if he wakes. The countdown begins, and at zero, I'm transported into the first scene of the movie. We're on a deserted beach, and I see a man frantically swimming to the shore. When he reaches it, he collapses on the sand, breathing heavily. A booted foot lands on his chest. I look up to see an officer in military uniform smirking down at the man on the ground. It's Barton Muir. In his characteristic drawl, he says, "Well, well, well. What have we here?"

I find myself entranced by the action, a story of espionage, intrigue and love that keeps my attention all the way to the end. Throughout the movie, I'm aware of Tobias's presence as an observer beside me. He's quiet, not interrupting the flow of the story, which I appreciate. When the final credits appear, I turn on the lights and blink, bringing myself back to my present reality.

"What did you think?" asks Tobias.

"I'm giving it five out five stars. How about you?"

Tobias cocks his head to one side, considering. "That's fair. I might deduct half a star for the unrealistic portrayal of the army general. He was a two-dimensional baddie who could have done with a little more nuance."

"Yeah, you're right, but it didn't detract from the main story, I felt." I yawn, suddenly feeling drained.

"I should let you get to bed."

"Thanks for this, Tobias. I had fun."

He nods solemnly. "Me too. I'll see you Tuesday, Viva. Goodnight."

"Goodnight." I end the call and haul myself out of the armchair. On the way to my room, I give Joe one final check. He's fast asleep, his arms up over his head in little fists, which is how he's slept since he was a baby. I let myself out of his room quietly and go to my bed. As I get under the covers, my mind turns to Tobias again. Tuesday can't come soon enough is my last thought as I sink into exhausted sleep.

Chapter 9

Tobias

I decide to bring Viva to my home, and not the penthouse. Something about my previous encounters with ladies from the agency has tainted the idea of entertaining Viva there. I don't want any parallels drawn between her and them. This is something entirely different, though what it is exactly I can't say yet.

I've had my chef prepare a wide selection of dishes, not knowing what cuisines Viva prefers. In many ways, we hardly know each other, but that's just the surface details. I haven't got this far in business without knowing how to read a person's character. I've had two years to get a read on Viva. In the ways that matter, I know her. Like, for example, I know that fundamentally, she's a giver. Every day in her work, she gives something of herself. That thing she does, where she channels her comforting vibes into you. I can sense her doing it, and the result speaks for itself. There have been times I've come to her feeling ragged and bitter from the events of my day, and somehow, magically, I've left her treatment room energized and content.

She does that not just for me, but all her other clients. I know, because I made sure to ask around before I first went to Sensual Healing, wanting to know who was their best master healer. I had my people discreetly question their regular clients, and the name most often on their lips was Viva. When I booked my first treatment, I specifically asked for her. The manager tried to fob me off on another person, but I insisted.

I'm home now, waiting for her arrival. Home is an eight-bedroom house in Great Neck, on twelve acres of private and highly secure grounds overlooking Manhasset Bay. I receive a notification on my communicator the minute the drone she's on flies into my protected airspace. By the time it lands on the forecourt of my house, I'm already out the door, waiting for her. She emerges from the drone, looking at her surroundings with stunned eyes. A panoply of lights illuminate the house and grounds like a beacon in the darkness of the late November evening. Then she catches sight of me. Trying to keep an impassive face, she walks towards me.

"Hey," she says.

"Hey," I parrot, momentarily unable to formulate any other words. Then, enough common sense returns for me to usher her into my house. "Come on inside," I say. She follows me up the front steps and into the large lobby dominated by a majestic circular staircase.

Again, she looks around in awe. "Wow, that's quite a place you got there."

I try to look at it with fresh eyes, like she would. "It is," I agree. "Let me take your coat."

She undoes the clasp of her coat and hands it to me, together with her scarf and hat. Temperatures haves dipped to wintry levels these past few days. I place them on the hook next to my own coat, finding a pleasing symmetry in the two clothing items next to each other. She hovers uncertainly behind me. I smile over my shoulder and indicate the bench she can sit on to take off her boots. I too remove the shoes I slipped on to go outside in. There is no need for shoes or slippers inside my home. The entire floor surface is covered with vantex, another trademark invention of mine. It's an easy-to-clean antibacterial flooring that looks and feels to the touch like plush carpet, with zero carbon heating technology built into it.

Wherever I walk in my house, my bare feet sink into soft, hygienic warmth. I have it in my offices too.

I take her hand. "Come on." I lead her to my favorite room in the house. Its floor-to-ceiling windows overlook the bay, though there's not much to see in the darkened evening. A great fireplace stands in pride of place at one end, a log fire crackling and exuding its pleasant resinous aroma. In the middle of the room are two sets of malleable armchairs and one long malleable couch placed around a rectangular coffee table, which at the touch of a button raises and spreads out to double up as a dining table. I spend a lot of time in this room—eat, meditate, read, you name it.

Along one wall are handcrafted oak bookshelves filled with physical books. I like to read on my communicator like any other person—it's practical and easy—but I cherish these books, many of them signed first editions by my best-loved contemporary and classic authors. Another wall is covered in a mural by the artist Levio, the same one who designed the dragon tattoo on my chest. This one depicts a wild forest glade and two people standing with their backs to us. The man and the woman are naked, holding hands, their hair long and free. It's art that can be interpreted whichever way you want. For me when I look at it, I see myself and my mate in an alternate life where we stand together as we battle for subsistence. It's fanciful thinking, even for me. However, I like the comfort it brings to see a depiction of myself in a different life where instead of being blessed with all material things but alone, I'm stripped to the most basic elements but have a partner.

Viva and I stand hand in hand, facing the mural, our stance mirroring that of the two people portrayed in it. She examines it a moment. "That's beautiful," she says. "Two soulmates facing up to the world together."

I gaze at her curiously. "Is that what you see?"

"Yes, isn't that what most others see?"

I shrug. "Not many have been here to see it, but mostly people think it's a depiction of Adam and Eve exiled from the Garden of Eden."

She looks at it again and scrunches her face. "It could be, I guess, but I prefer my first interpretation."

"Yeah, I prefer it too."

She turns and peruses the rest of the room. Her eyes light up at the sight of the bookshelves. She walks over to them, running her fingers lightly along the spines of the books, reading the titles. "War and Peace," she smiles. "I read that in three days; couldn't put it down. Paid for it with a spasmic neck and shoulders for days afterwards." She moves on, humming under her breath as she examines the contents of my library. "A Tale of Two Cities," she murmurs. "My favourite Dickens." She walks on, smiling as she sees the Harry Potter series. "I loved these growing up," she says. She moves on, reaching the more contemporary section of books. "Maxine Drake!" she exclaims delightedly. "I love all her books."

"There's a new one out next month. I have an early copy, if you want to read it."

She swivels to face me, her eyes twinkling in amusement. "A pre-release of the latest Barton Muir, now an early copy of Maxine Drake. What next?"

I laugh shortly. "Anything you want, Viva. I guarantee I can get hold of it."

"Must be quite something to be able to get your hands on anything you want," she muses.

"Not anything," I say gruffly.

"Oh really? What has eluded you?"

I place my hands loosely around her waist. "I've spent weeks craving you, Viva."

She touches her palm to my chest, as if feeling the pounding of my heart. "I'm here now," she says softly. "What you gonna do about it?"

"This," I say, and pull her to me, capturing her lips with mine. This kiss is nothing like the one we shared last Friday. That had been restrained, tender, sweet. Now, having her here in my space, I unleash my hunger, running my hands through her long, ebony hair to hold her in place as I ravage her lips. She parts them in response, allowing my tongue to enter and taste her. She tastes good, better than good. I lap her up, letting my tongue roll over hers, wanting to be inside her in any way that I can. I had plans for us to eat first, fuck later, but I'm going to need to re-arrange them. Being a plain-spoken man, I give it to her straight. "I need to fuck you now, Viva. Can't wait."

She stares breathlessly at me, her brown eyes heavy with desire. "Do it," she says.

Chapter 10

Viva

Tobias leads me towards a semi-concealed staircase off one corner of the room. His palm engulfs my much smaller hand, giving me a heady sense of security that I never dreamt I would need. I mean, I'm an independent, modern woman. I can take care of myself. But it's nice, having him hold my hand.

"This takes us up to my bedroom," he says with slight smile. "It's separate from all the other upstairs rooms."

"So, if you have visitors, they're not in your space."

"I don't get many visitors, but yes. Whenever my sister stays over, I can almost entirely avoid her." He says that with an ironic roll of his eyes. I get it. Family isn't always what it's cracked up to be. That said, I'm one of the lucky ones, having a mom I truly get on with.

"Neat," I reply. "You designed this house yourself?"

"Yes, with the help of an architect friend of mine. I wanted everything to be just right."

We've reached the top of the stairs. Before us is a large bedroom with the same floor-to-ceiling windows as below. He must wake up to an amazing view each morning. The room is decorated in cool, neutral tones. The gray vantex flooring is in a shade not dissimilar to his eyes. The walls are a pale apple green. A large bed takes up one wall space, laid with satin sheets of a dark teal shade of green.

My inspection is cut short as Tobias turns me to face him. He takes my face in his hands and kisses me. When he pulls back, he says roughly, "We can talk later, Viva.

Now, I want you naked." With that, he tugs at my sweater and pulls it over my head. Under it I'm wearing my pale lavender tunic, my uniform at Sensual Healing. That too, is quickly dispensed with, leaving me in a form-fitting nude bra. With expert hands, he unclasps and throws it to the floor. Those same hands come back to cup my breasts, unabashedly admiring them. "Gorgeous, simply gorgeous," he says, his thumbs running circles over my nipples.

He raises his gaze to me. "You've had many chances to ogle me, Viva, now it's my turn to return the favor." He brings his hands to the elasticated waist of my pants and pulls them down to my feet, together with my panties. I help kick them away. He sits back on his knees, taking in the sight of me naked. I let him look his fill. It's not like I'm shy about my body. I keep in shape—hard not to with the physical work I do. Before I had Joe, when I could afford to spend money on myself, I went for a permanent hair removal treatment. My legs are silky smooth, my pussy bare except for an artful heart-shaped patch on my pubic mound.

"Mmm," murmurs Tobias, stroking his hands up my thighs, teasing my pussy before continuing to my belly button. "I knew your skin would feel like satin, pretty girl." His hands circle round to my back, then down, grasping each cheek of my ass, spreading them out.

My core is wet and needy. "Touch me there," I plead.

"All in good time." This is payback for the times I've kept him waiting, edged him to the point of frustration, before finally putting my hands to his cock. "Turn around," he commands. I do as he asks. His hands slide up the back of my thighs, then higher, teasing circles around my ass. "Lean down with your elbows on the bed," he issues softly. I bend over and place my elbows on the satiny sheet, my ass sticking out behind me. His face comes in to nuzzle me.

"Ah," he sighs. "So good." He runs his lips over the generous curves of my buttocks, coming to a halt at the crease in the center and placing a kiss there. "So fucking good."

"Tobias," I moan, desperate for his touch.

"When I'm good and ready, baby, when I'm good and ready."

For the next few minutes, he meanders over my thighs, my ass cheeks, my lower back, sliding his hands over my skin and following with a trail of soft kisses. My aching pussy, he leaves alone, except for small, incidental little touches that light me on fire. I'm sure he can see how wet I am for him.

I feel him give me a little push. "Move forward on the bed, Viva, and bring your knees up." Soon, I'm lying on my front with my knees bent under me. He spreads my legs wide. For a long moment, he simply looks while I feel the touch of the cool air on my heated skin. Then he buries his face between my legs and begins a series of wet, sloppy kisses all over—on the rosebud of my ass, the folds of my pussy, my clit, the inside of my thighs, my ass cheeks. I feel him squeeze the soft, squishy flesh and then he's biting it and sucking, making sure to leave his mark.

"Tobias," I groan. "Please."

"Is that what you want?" He licks me long and slow from my clit to my slit.

"Oh yeah," I pant.

"You got it." He kisses my pussy, flicking his tongue back and forth.

"Ah."

Now that he's got down to business, there's no more messing around, no more teasing. He eats my pussy with open-mouthed kisses and steady licks of his clever tongue, driving me to the edge but careful not to let me go over it.

My face buried in the sheets, I close my eyes and let go, giving in to the enjoyment of his leisurely seduction. He takes his sweet time, seemingly happy to linger over my delicate folds, worshipping them with his mouth and tongue.

I'm jolted from my trance when he lifts his lips away and mutters, "Move forward on the bed." I shuffle forwards. "More," he barks. I move myself further along until my face lands on his pillow, breathing the residual musky scent left on there. I feel him get on the bed behind me. Turning my head, I see him position himself on his back, his feet still on the floor. Our eyes meet. "Fuck my face with your pussy, Viva," he rasps. He helps lift me over him, rearranging his position until his face is under me, his lips perfectly placed to eat my pussy. I raise my hips slightly and begin to swing them back and forth over his searching tongue. Oh, that feels good.

With my face buried in his pillow, letting his masculine scent surround me, I chase my orgasm, rubbing my slick pussy over his hungry mouth. Over and over, I pleasure myself on his tongue, uncaring of anything except finding my release. When it comes, it hits me like a giant wave. I give a cry as my body explodes into thousands of pulsing contractions which seem to go on and on and on. Exhausted, I collapse over him. I feel him gently lift my hips and disengage himself, but I'm too languid to do anything except lie prone, face still buried in his fragrant pillow.

Beside me I hear the rustling sound of clothes being removed, then a drawer being opened and something taken out of it. With an effort, I turn my head to the side and open my eyes. He's holding in his hand some kind of sex toy with a life sized dildo attached to it. "This is made exactly to the shape of my cock," he says. With a grin, he adds, "Much as I wish, I can't be in two places at once, but this is the next best thing. I'm going to fuck you with my two cocks, Viva, one in your pussy and one in your mouth. You got a problem with that?"

"None," I breathe.

"Good girl," he purrs. "Turn around and lie on your back."

I follow his instruction and watch as he sets up the sex toy on its mechanical legs and slants the dildo so it's at my opening. He presses a button on a remote device, and a springing mechanism pushes the dildo forward into my pussy, very slowly. "How does that feel?" he asks.

"It's good."

"You want it deeper?"

"Maybe a little."

He adjusts something on the dildo and now it's thrusting slowly all the way to the hilt. "Good?"

"Yeah."

"Okay, let me change the speed." He presses something else on the device and suddenly, the fake cock in my pussy is driving in and out at a much faster, though not a frantic pace.

I sigh. "That's good."

With a smile, he straddles my body, bending down to brush a kiss over my lips. "Ready to take my cock?"

"I've been dreaming of it for months."

"Oh yeah?" He looks pleased. "Viva, I've been dreaming of it for years." And with that, he taps his shaft to my bottom lip. "Open up," he commands.

I take an exploratory lick, running my tongue around the glistening tip. "Suck it, Viva." His tone brooks no disobedience. I open my mouth and take a few inches in, sucking deeply. "Ah, that's good," he praises. He lets me suck for a few minutes longer, then pulls away. "I want you to relax your throat, Viva, and let me all the way in. You don't have to do anything other than take me and let me fuck your mouth. Think you can do that?"

"I'll try," I mumble.

"If you want me to stop, smack my thigh. Okay?"

"Okay."

"Open up wide, Viva. Breathe through your nose."

I do as he says, feeling him slowly push his way deep into my throat. "Look how well you take me," he whispers.

I feel so full, both my pussy and my mouth filled with his cock. All I can do is look at him, tears welling in my eyes. He pulls away slowly and then he's back, all the way down my throat. "Good girl," he purrs, looking so proud of me. Starting with small pulses at first, he begins to fuck my mouth, consciously following the same rhythm as the cock thrusting in my pussy. It's uncomfortable at first, but gradually, I feel myself lean into it and relaxing. Throughout, my eyes are locked on his. He moans his pleasure and showers me with praise. "Such a good girl, Viva. You feel so fucking good." I get lost in the moment, stuffed with cock and high on praise.

He must have touched the controls on the device again, because all of a sudden, the cock in my pussy is thrusting fast, and his cock in my mouth is matching its pace. "I'm close," he grunts. "Are you gonna come for me?"

I moan around his cock. I don't know. I've never done something like this before. Am I going to come? Maybe. He's fucking me hard now, and with each thrust, grits out, "You liked the taste of my cum, didn't you Viva. You gonna drink me again? I know you want to. You're gonna take every last drop like a good girl, aren't you?" He taps on his device and now, there's something fluttering over my clit. I wish I could have a sex toy like this at home, I think fleetingly. But I don't linger on the thought as my mind goes haywire, in the grip of intense sensation. Tobias's face above me is set in a near grimace. "You better come right now, Viva," he hisses.

On the next thrust, I convulse, moaning around his cock. A moment later, he gives a guttural cry and his cum gushes into my throat. He pulls away, letting me swallow. I can barely think as my mouth is awash with his intensely musky flavor. I try to swallow it all, but some of it leaks out of my mouth. In his dirtiest, sexiest move so far, Tobias licks the escaping fluid and gifts it back to me in a deep, hungry kiss. He hasn't switched off the device, so I'm still being pounded by the dildo cock with the fluttering on my clit as he kisses me, his hands holding my face firmly. Unbelievably, another wave of contractions grips me. I moan into his mouth and he releases me on a panting breath. Gently, he brushes a stray strand of hair from my face, looking into my eyes, approval warming his gaze. "I just knew it," he says softly. "You were made for taking my cock, Viva."

Then he taps the device to stop its movement and ever so gently pulls it out of me. He bends down to press a soft kiss on my throbbing, aching pussy. "Stay there," he says. "I'll start the bath." He gets to his feet and heads to the adjoining bathroom while I close my eyes, utterly drained. Distantly, I hear the sound of water, but I'm too tired to move. I've had my fair share of sex, ranging from the so-so to the spectacular, but something as epic as this, I've never experienced before. Bastard. Not only is he rich and sinfully sexy, now I know he fucks like a pro. A semi-hysterical giggle escapes my throat as I realize. He hasn't even fucked me yet.

"What's so funny?" he asks, re-entering the room.

"I was just thinking. All this, and he hasn't even properly fucked me yet."

His face lights up with a smile. "I will, Viva, I will. You won't be going home before I've put my cock in your pussy. But first things first. Let's get in the bath."

He takes my hands and pulls me up to sitting then to my feet. He doesn't let me go at first, looking down at me, an unreadable expression on his face. Then he pushes aside whatever thought he's thinking and kisses me softly. "Come on." Hand in hand, we walk to his bathroom. At the threshold, I stop and stare in awe. Of course, he wouldn't have a normal, ordinary sort of bathroom. This room is massive, and the bath more like a shallow pool than a tub. It's full to the brim with steaming water. The bath sits beside another enormous window looking out to the sea. God what a view it must be in daylight.

Grinning, Tobias points to the bottle of bath salts with the Sensual Healing logo on it, which is sitting on the side of the tub. "I'm giving you the master healer experience, except in reverse."

"I don't think I've ever given my clients three orgasms on the trot and double penetration," I say in riposte.

"And you better not unless it's me," he growls. I take his proffered hand and climb into the bath, sighing in relief as my aching body is submerged in heat. He follows me in, settling himself behind me. With a press of a button, he activates light vibration in the water, then pulls me to him so my head rests on his chest.

"Ah, this is the life," I murmur.

"It's good; I can't complain."

We repose in silence, letting the bath salts and hot vibrating water around us do their healing magic. I let my thoughts wander.

"Why are you still single?" I ask out of the blue.

"Why do you ask?" he retorts.

"It's just, well… It's easy to understand why I'm single. I have a young child, I've been badly burned by my ex, my life is all about my boy now and everything else takes second place. But you? You have it all. You're rich, gorgeous, clever and sexy. Kind and generous too. Add to that you know how to please a woman in bed. You're a catch, Tobias. You could take your pick of women. So why are you alone?"

He twirls a stray lock of my hair around his finger. "Have you ever thought that I might have been badly burned too? It's no secret I've been married before and it didn't end well. I'm not doing that ever again."

I turn my head to face him. "So what, you're going to go through life without companionship just because your ex-wife was a bitch?"

His mouth twists at my choice of word about his ex. "The problem is, Viva, that she wasn't a bitch before we married; at least it wasn't apparent to me. You'd be surprised the lengths people will go to in order to have access to the kind of wealth I have. And the other problem is that the good women who are not interested in my money find my wealth obscene and therefore avoid me like the plague."

I'm silent a moment, digesting this information. Then I have to ask, "So what camp am I in, according to you? Am I in the 'would go to any lengths to get your money' or 'wouldn't touch a man of your wealth with a bargepole' camp?"

"I can't say," he answers, sounding aloof.

"I'm not interested in your money, Tobias," I reply, a little stung.

"That's what they all say."

I feel a chill that has nothing to do with the temperature of the water. On some level, I can understand where he's coming from. There's lots of money-hungry people out there, and he's right to be on his guard. However, I dislike my motives and good character being put in question. I know we're not actually dating, just hanging out in private once a week, but still... Can I share my time and my body with someone who so blatantly distrusts me?

All at once, doubts creep in about what we're doing here. Maybe it might be best if, as soon as we've eaten dinner, I make my excuses and go home. Then at leisure I can think things through and decide the best way forward.

The silence has gone on a little too long, so I give a nonchalant shrug. "Fair enough," I tell him. Changing the subject, I add, "Are you planning to feed me soon? I'm hungry."

His chuckles, "Dinner will be waiting for us downstairs, just as soon as we get out of here."

I make to stand. "Well then, what are we waiting for?"

He stops me with his hand. "Viva, look at me."

I twist around with a look of enquiry. He hesitates a moment. Finally, he asks, "Are we good?"

"Sure," I smile.

"Don't give me that shit!" he exclaims, looking annoyed. "I felt you freeze me out just now."

"Tobias," I say, trying to maintain my cool. "I get where you're coming from, I do. But you just basically said you don't trust my motives for being with you. I have to tell you that puts a dampener on things."

He huffs. "It's not that I distrust you, Viva, but being around the kind of money I have... It can have a corrupting influence on people. After a while, it can distort things. Make you want to put up with me, even if I no longer attract you, just so you can dine in style and enjoy all this."

I sigh. "And we're back to square one. Your trust levels are low. I get it. I'm hardly one to talk when I don't have that great a trust in men myself. I guess it's something I'll need to factor in when thinking about how we go forward from here. But let's not argue over it now. Come on. Time to feed me."

He relents and lets me go.

Chapter 11

Tobias

We're back downstairs, dressed in bathrobes, and looking at the veritable feast that my chef has prepared for us. Viva takes it all in and asks wryly, "Were you expecting more than one person for company tonight?"

"I wasn't sure what you liked, so I thought is best to have a wide selection," I reply.

"That's sweet," she smiles. "For the avoidance of future doubts, Tobias, I'm easy. There's very little I won't eat. Super-spicy I can just about tolerate, and I'm not very keen on pickles, but apart from that, I'm good."

"Noted. Now what will you have?"

She takes the plate from me. "I'll try some of those dumplings. And is that rare steak?"

"It is."

"Well, can't have such luxuries go to waste. I'll have some of that too, with the sauteed vegetables."

I serve her plate with generous portions of each, adding melt-in-your-mouth gratin potatoes to the mix. She takes the plate from me with a gracious smile and perches herself beside me on the malleable couch. I watch her take her first bite of food and chew thoughtfully. She catches my look. "It's good," she assures me with a smile. "Thank you."

I serve myself and we eat in silence for some minutes. Despite our talk earlier, or maybe because of it, I sense she's withdrawn from me. I curse myself. Why the fuck did

I have to go and ruin the moment? Well, but she was the one to ask the question. All I did was give her an honest answer. Truly, I don't distrust Viva. I know she's good and kind, a giving person. But I've seen what being around money can do to people. It's more that I distrust future Viva, once she's gotten used to the luxuries I can give her. And I know that's a shitty way to think about it, but it's my truth right now.

We talk a little as we eat, but it's stilted, as if a barrier has come down between us. It's clear we're not returning to the bedroom any time soon for some follow up action. What pisses me off the most, however, is Viva being on guard with me. I'm not blind to the irony that it's my own guarded attitude that has made her take a step back from me. I need to do something to break the ice, else she'll go home and overthink things, and before I know it, she'll have called this whole thing off. I'm not having that happen.

She puts her fork down on her empty plate. "That was delicious, Tobias. Thanks for this."

I know she's about to excuse herself and go home. Time to pull in the big guns. "Viva," I growl. "Come here."

"Huh?" She looks at me, surprised.

I pat my thighs. "Here," I say.

Hesitantly, she comes to me. Putting my arms around her, I easily bring her much smaller frame into my lap. I envelop her in my embrace, my arms and legs bracketing her. Once she's securely nestled in my warmth, I bend my head down and whisper into her ear. "Relax, Viva. Let me hold you."

Wrong words. I know only too well that being told to relax often has the opposite effect. I backtrack and start again. "Viva, don't you fucking freeze me out. I'm going to say some truths to you, lay everything on the line so we both know where we stand. First and most important of all, I'm crazy about you. I've obsessed about you since maybe our first meeting. Why else do you think I got so messed up when you weren't there two weeks ago? So don't you dare call this thing off because you've got cold feet all of a sudden. I need you too much, and I think—no, I know—you need me too." I feel her tremble in my arms, so I tighten my hold on her and rain kisses along her neck and jaw.

"Second thing I want to say. Viva, I trust you. You wouldn't be here if I didn't. I want you to know you are the first female, other than family, to have come to my house. I'm a very private man, and I allow very few people into my sanctuary. You're here because I know you and I trust you. Period."

She twists in my arms to put her hand to my cheek and drop a kiss on my lips. "I suppose you should know I trust you too," she murmurs. "I don't do this kind of thing with anyone. I haven't dated for a very long time."

"Since when?" I demand.

She snorts. "About two years ago."

"Figures. Last time I had sex with anyone, apart from our little interlude earlier on, was close on two years ago."

She's quiet, eyes searching mine. "Is that simply a coincidence?"

I scoff. "Hardly. It means we fell for each other two years ago, but have been too dumb to do anything about it."

"Well, in my defence, Tobias, I did have a job to protect."

I kiss the tip of her nose. "I'll rephrase. *I* was too dumb to do anything about it."

She rubs her lips over mine. "That's better," she concurs.

I capture those sweet lips and spend a long time thoroughly kissing her. Afterwards, she snuggles tight in my arms again, and I resume the conversation. "Third thing. I said it badly before, so I want to explain again. I worry, Viva, about being taken for a ride again, and that's not to say I think you'll do that, but it would be good to acknowledge that the fear is there."

She presses my hand. "I understand."

"I want you to please, please promise me something. That you'll only ever be with me because you want me. Anytime that changes, I need to know. And even if we go our separate ways, I'll make sure you're financially set up for life, you and Joe."

She goes to protest. "I don't want your money—"

"I know, Viva, I know. Again, I'm handling this badly. I want to take care of you, but you're an independent person, I get it. Just know, you don't need to be with me to get me to give you money. I'll gladly give it if ever you ask."

"I won't," she answers spiritedly.

"Okay," I say. I nuzzle her neck. "Will you stay the night, please?"

"As long as I'm back home by seven so I can have breakfast with Joe before he goes to school."

"I'll make sure the drone gets you back on time."

"Okay then," she breathes.

"So, one more question I have for you. Are you protected?"

She gives a short laugh. "Let's put it this way, Tobias. Much as I love Joe, I ain't ever getting accidentally pregnant again."

"Good to know. I'm fully vaccinated, by the way."

"So, we're good."

"We're good." I grind my hips into her ass, making her feel my hard length. "Viva, I want you to sit your pretty pussy on my cock."

"Yes, sir," comes her smart reply. Nimbly, she turns her body around to straddle mine. I look down at the knotted tie of her robe. Without words, she undoes it and lets the robe flap open, gifting me with the sight of her lovely naked breasts. I bend my head and pay homage to each tip with my mouth.

"Ride my cock, Viva," I growl.

With a wicked smile, she shifts forward and slowly lowers herself onto my swollen shaft. It takes a few tries before I'm fully sheathed inside her. Her eyes are level with mine, so are her lips. I can't resist another taste of her. I plunge my tongue inside her mouth and take a good long taste. I break the kiss and bring my hands down to cup her ass. "Ride me," I say again.

Leaning her hands on my shoulders for balance, she starts bouncing gently on my cock, finding the rhythm that suits her. All the while, I watch her beautiful face, which is scrunched in concentration as she focuses on her pleasure. When I sense her tiring, I take over, punching my groin up into hers. "Touch yourself," I bark. She brings her hand down to her clit, circling it with two fingers. "That's my good girl," I tell her breathlessly as I strain with all my might to thrust up into her tight pussy. "Come for me, Viva."

"I'm nearly there," she pants.

With my feet planted firmly on the floor, I drive up into her, over and over. "Let me feel you come," I grunt. I'm desperate to spill my seed inside her, and it's taking a supreme effort to hold back. *Come on, Viva.* My eyes lock onto hers and I know, before even feeling it on my cock, the exact moment when it happens. Her doe eyes widen and lose focus. She cries out, and then her cunt is strangling my cock with wave after wave of tight convulsions. With a hoarse cry, I drive one last time into her and shoot my cum.

We come to a rest, still joined intimately. I pull her to me and just hold her in my embrace for a very long time, waiting for my pounding heart to slow down to its normal beat. Our moment is interrupted by a call on her communicator. Hurriedly, she lifts herself off me and ties her robe, then grabs the device from her pocket. With a double tap on the screen, she accepts the call. From where I'm sitting, I catch a glimpse of a young, dark-haired boy. "Momma," he cries.

"Hey, sweet boy. Are you having fun at Grandma's?"

He nods excitedly. "Ben came over and we played Koondles," he says happily.

I'm not exactly au fait with what Koondles is, but I must assume it's some type of kids' game. Viva beams at him. "How nice! Did you play fairly, each taking turns?"

He sighs exaggeratedly. "Yes, Mom." Then he leans forward, looking closely at the screen. "Mom, why are you in a bathrobe?"

She looks down at herself. "Oh this? It's because I just took a bath."

"But your bathrobe is different."

She smiles. "I borrowed this one from my friend."

"What friend?" asks Joe suspiciously.

"The friend I'm visiting tonight. He's called Tobias."

He frowns in concentration. "Don't know anyone called Tobias."

"No, that's right, Joe. You haven't met him, but he's a friend I know from work."

"Where is he?"

She nods towards me. "Right here."

"Hello, Tobias!" he calls out.

Viva lifts an enquiring brow at me. With a smile, I lean sideways to come into the screen's view. "Hello, Joe. It's nice to meet you."

He stares then asks, "Did you have a bath too?"

"I did," I say evenly.

Joe smiles. "Me too. Now we're all ready for bed."

That we are. "Goodnight, Joe," I say.

"G'night, Tobias."

Viva blows her son a kiss. "Goodnight, sweet boy."

"Night, Mom."

They end the call shortly after. I look at her. "You heard what he said. Time to go to bed." I stand and pull her to her feet. She glances at the food plates still on the table, but I shake my head. "My staff will take care of this. Let's go." Hand in hand, we walk upstairs to my room.

Chapter 12

Viva

I come awake slowly, aware of being somewhere different to my usual. My head nestles on silky soft material, and the pillow is a little plumper than the one I have at home. In a rush, memories of last night come flooding back. I force my groggy eyes open. It's still dark outside, the night light on the wall illuminating the room with a faint glow. I'm curled up on my side clutching a spare pillow, just the way I like. I remember Tobias's amusement at seeing the way I settle down to sleep. It's a long-standing habit of mine. I just find it comforting to hug a pillow; plus it provides support for my spine. *Maybe you should try hugging a person instead.* The unbidden thought comes to me as I watch Tobias. He's lying on his side too, fast asleep, his face inches from mine.

As I try to chase the ridiculous thought away, I realize my left leg is entangled with one of his. *How about I hug both the pillow and him?* Another wayward thought from my sleepy mind. I study his face in repose. He looks younger, more vulnerable somehow, the dark soot of his lashes forming a thick curtain below his eyes. I shuffle my body gently towards him and let the arm that's currently hugging a pillow reach over and rest on his side, just above his waist. My head now rests on his pillow, our faces so close that I can rub my nose to his. *That's much better.*

Tobias murmurs unintelligibly and brings his free arm over my side, easing me closer into his embrace. I feel his warm hand stroke along my back.

"Mmm," I mumble.

"Mmm," he rumbles in return. Then, without opening his eyes, "Athena, time."

The disembodied voice from his communicator responds, "It is five fifteen."

"Athena, wake us up at six."

"Understood."

He pulls me close. "Sleep, Viva." And so, miraculously, I do.

I'm woken again by the gentle hum of a melody playing softly at my side. *"That's nice,"* says a sleepy thought in my head. The music is interrupted by a voice that speaks quietly, "It is six AM." Then the music resumes.

"Mmm," I mumble.

"Mmm," Tobias rumbles. "You can have the bathroom first."

"In a minute." It's too cozy where I am to want to move. I drift off again.

All too soon, Athena chides us again. "It is five minutes past six." Is it me, or is her voice a little louder than before? The music comes back on.

Tobias brushes his lips over my cheek. "We need to get up," he murmurs.

"Yeah," I concur.

His hand moves from around my waist and begins a slow exploration of my body, slipping under the shirt he loaned me for sleeping in and stroking the skin of my lower back, the swell of my ass, up to my breasts before finally coming down to rest on my pussy. He cups my mound with his palm, as if laying claim to it. Then his fingers begin a leisurely stroke of my clit.

"Ah, that's nice," I breathe.

"Very," he agrees.

I don't move, but simply bask in his comforting embrace and sensual touch. Athena speaks to us again, telling us it is ten past six. "Athena, stop," Tobias says, and blessedly all goes quiet. He continues to caress my clit, occasionally dipping his fingers in my wet folds to lubricate them before returning to his task.

"I should warn you, I could have you do this for hours," I say, my voice still husky from sleep.

"I'm happy to, although I promised to get you home by seven."

"Yeah," I sigh. "What time do I need to leave?"

"We have another twenty minutes to spend in bed."

"Okay." I go quiet, enjoying the arousing yet simultaneously calming touch of his fingers on my clit. Truly, this is heaven. My mind travels back to all the delicious things this man did to me last night. After we went to bed, he spent at least an hour worshipping my body, bringing me to the edge time and time again before finally letting me have it as he fucked me hard to a glorious climax. My core throbs in memory of it. As if sensing my heightened state of arousal, his fingers gather speed as they stroke me over and over. I make a little moaning sound in the back of my throat. *Yes, there, just there. Keep going.* I speak to him in my head and it's as if he hears me. His fingers work their magic on my engorged nub. "Mmm," I moan deeply, and convulse in pulse after pulse of sweet pleasure.

When I'm done, he removes his hand, bringing the wet fingers to his lips. His eyes are hazy with lust. "Feel me," he rasps, guiding my hand to his hardened cock. I squeeze it, marvelling at the soft texture and steely strength. His lips find mine. In between kisses, he mutters, "You're going to leave here with my cum in your pussy. All day, Viva, you're going to feel it dripping into your panties. While you put your hands on other men's cocks and pleasure them, it will be my cum inside you and my cock you'll think about." His words send a delicious thrill through me. He sounds jealous and possessive, and oh God why does it turn me on?

I feel bound to make a token protest. "During a treatment, I focus all my attention on a client. I have to keep that connection open and channel my loving energy, otherwise it doesn't work."

"I know," he says, sounding gruff, "but thoughts of me will seep through. Let them turn you on, and then you can channel all that turned on energy on whichever lucky client happens to be with you."

"Yes," I say, knowing it will be impossible to keep my mind from thinking of him.

"Now, come here and let me fuck you." He positions himself over me, and in an instant plunges deep inside. He starts a rapid rhythm. We're short on time, so I know this is going to be a quickie. Even so, I feel every single thrust of his cock, the nerve endings in my core still throbbing from my recent release. He pistons into me, his face set in concentration. I'm riveted, watching him find his release. He groans, pressing his shaft deep inside me, as he showers my womb with his cum.

He takes a moment or two to regain his breath, then he bends over me, elbows at my side. In a reverse of his earlier passion, he kisses me softly and laughs. "That's quite a way to wake up in the morning."

"I can't complain." Then I speak the niggling thought that's been bothering me. "Tobias, do you mind about the work I do? The fact that I touch others intimately?"

He huffs. "Yes, I do mind. I'm not going to say I like the thought of you jerking other men's cocks."

"It's all done very professionally," I'm quick to say.

His smile is rueful. "I know how professional you are, Viva. And I know that this is the job you do to put food on the table for you and Joe, and also that you're fiercely proud and independent. I won't waste my breath trying to get you to give it up. Besides, I can't begrudge these other men and women the opportunity to experience the magic you weave. You're special, Viva. You give people the most intense sense of relaxation and bliss. It's a gift, and it would be selfish of me to only want it for myself. I can make my peace with that as long as nobody lays a finger on you."

I stroke his cheek, which is rough with stubble. "Only you are allowed to touch me," I say softly.

He kisses my hand. "Then we're good." Reluctantly, he pulls out of me, saying, "We better make a move. Can you wash and dress in five?"

"I can." I sit up, feeling a wet gush flow down my thighs.

He sees it too and smirks, "No washing that off, though."

I shake my head at him and hurry to the bathroom. When I come out again a few minutes later, I find my clothes, freshly laundered, laid on the bed for me. There's also a steaming cup of coffee next to a note that says, "Meet me downstairs when you're done. T." With a dreamy smile, I dress and slurp down my coffee. Then I'm hurrying down. I find him sitting on a malleable chair, reading something on his communicator. He puts it away and stands, holding out his hand to me. There's only time to have a brief look at the glorious view over the water, visible now it's daylight, before he's ushering me out and over to the entrance lobby. I pull on my boots, coat, hat and scarf, then I'm ready to face the elements. He's in casual pants and a sweater, like yesterday. "You don't have to come outside," I tell him.

He tuts, ignoring my comment, and leads me out the front door. The drone is waiting for me in the same space where it dropped me last night. He walks me to its door, then kisses me briskly. "I'll see you Friday, Viva, six o'clock as usual."

"See you then. Thank you, for everything."

I climb aboard, fasten my seatbelt, and watch as his house soon becomes a spot on the horizon. I make it to Mom's place a minute after seven, letting myself in through the door. Joe is already up, and greets me excitedly. "Momma!"

"Hey, sweet boy, have you been good for Grandma?"

Mom answers for him. "He has, except for a little tantrum at bedtime with wanting another story." *I know those well.*

"Come on," I say. "Let's get you dressed and how about we have pancakes for breakfast today?"

"Yes!" I take him up to his room, which Mom keeps for him whenever he stays at her place. We make quick work of getting him dressed. Then I leave him in the living room, settled in his virtual play space while I go make the pancakes.

In the kitchen, I find Mom nursing a cup of coffee. I decline her offer of a cup, saying, "No, it's okay. I've already had one this morning. I'll just get myself some juice." She watches me as I pour it in a glass and then set about preparing the pancakes.

"So, are you going to tell me how it went?" she enquires.

"It went well." I blush at the memory. "More than well."

She smiles. "I'm glad. But you'll be careful though, won't you?"

I go over to where she's sitting and give her a hug. "I'm being careful. Don't worry."

"I can't help it. It's a mother's lot to worry," she says wryly. "So, is this going to be a regular thing, once every week?"

I nod. "If you're okay looking after Joe."

"That's not a problem. You know it."

"Thanks, Mom."

She's still not satisfied. "But where is it going to lead? Are you just going to see him once a week until the end of time? How's that going to work for you?"

I shrug. "It works for now. I'm going to take it one day at a time. And whenever it stops working, then I'll reassess."

She snorts as she stands, but all she says is, "I'll go get Joe."

All day at work, I try to keep focused on my clients, but as Tobias predicted, thoughts of him keep straying into my consciousness. It doesn't help that I can still feel the sticky residue of his cum in my panties. I try my best, though, to do each client justice. They pay a lot for their treatments, and they deserve the best I can give them.

I finish early, which gives me time to go home, change, and then go pick up Joe from school. As I let myself in through the door of my apartment, I notice there's a parcel that's been left there for me. Curious, I pick it up, no clue on the label to show who has sent it. I peel away the packaging and look inside, a laugh escaping from me. Inside is the replica dildo of Tobias's cock and the contraption with the springing mechanism together with its activating device. There's a note too, old-fashionably handwritten, that says, "Use this whenever you feel the need for my cock inside you. I'll know the minute you activate it. T."

Chapter 13

Tobias

Work has kept me busy these last two days, which is no bad thing, stopping me as it has from dwelling too much on one person. Even so, Viva hasn't been far from my thoughts. I keep wondering what she's doing or thinking. Is she thinking of me? The arrogant side of me says yes.

I've had no word from her except for a brief message thanking me for my "gift". She hasn't yet used the dildo I sent her; I'll get an alert on my communicator whenever she does. I guess it's no surprise. I used her pussy well, and she's going to need a few days to recover. I can't help the pleased smirk that forms on my face.

"What was that?" asks Ralph.

"What?"

"That look on your face just now. You can't have been thinking of Mr Huo or the fact that Huotech Industries are in secret talks with Poladar Inc to try to get in bed with the Venorians before we do. Were you even listening to a word I just said?"

We're on board my supersonic jet on our way back from an interesting set of meetings with top Chinese representatives in the aerospace industry. They too have identified the opportunities presented by our first contact with the Venorians, but if they think they'll steal a march on me, then they're very much mistaken. Firstly, I already have the ground facilities and much of the expertise needed for my spaceship project to take off. And secondly, seeing as it was mostly my company that provided the know-how and materials for building the Mars space station, I have first dibs on any future trade negotiations with the Venorians.

"How much do I pay you, Ralph?" I say with a raised brow.

He looks amused, knowing where this is going. "Very generously, Tobias."

"And does the contract that comes with this generous salary package include your right to interrogate me on what I'm thinking?"

"It does not, but I was doing it in my capacity as your friend," he retorts.

I give him my death stare. "Do you have the temerity, Ralph, to call yourself my friend?"

He purses his lips, trying not to smile, damn him. "I do. I might even go as far as to say I'm your only friend."

This is getting beyond the pale. "Have a care, Ralph, for what you say," I murmur softly.

He continues breezily, "That smiling look I just saw wouldn't by any chance have anything to do with the fact it's Friday and we're due to land back home at five pm?"

"Ralph," I warn.

"Or the fact that since a certain someone got clearance to visit you last Tuesday, you've been breaking out into smiles at the oddest times."

"That's enough! I'm not discussing Viva with you or anyone else."

He finally relents, which is a relief as yes, he is my only friend, and I'd have to cut off my right arm before cutting him out of my life. With a nonchalant shrug, he grumbles, "Fine. I'll just say it's been a nice change not to have Mr Grumpy around the office this week."

"Noted. Now let's get back to business."

An hour later, we land and transfer to my waiting drone. There's just enough time for me to go to my office for a brief final meeting with my immediate staff, then I'm heading out to Sensual Healing. I stalk into the reception lobby, barely looking at the person working the desk before I'm heading towards Viva's door. She's there waiting for me with a warm smile. "Good evening, Mr Moore."

"Hello, Viva." I walk past her into the room, leaving my bodyguards to wait outside. She shuts the door behind me. I know what my usual routine entails. I'm supposed to undress, get into the spa bath then once I'm bathed, towel myself dry and go lie on the massage bed. We said we'd keep things professional when I'm here. I pace about, gearing myself up to do just that, but... *Fuck it.* In two strides, I have her pinned against the door, my mouth on hers. Oh, the relief of feeling her soft skin and to breathe her in. It's only now that I finally feel like I've come home. Alarm bells are going off in the back of my head that this thing is getting dangerously out of control. I ignore them and keep kissing her.

It's a long, long time before I pull back. She's panting breathlessly, her lips swollen from my kiss. She's so goddamn beautiful.

"I missed you," I say a little gruffly.

"I missed you too."

I see her take a deep breath, trying to get things back on track. I pre-empt whatever else she's about to say. With my thumb, I stroke her plump bottom lip and murmur, "I know we were going to keep things business-like here, and we will. I just needed to do this first."

"Okay," she says softly.

Reluctantly, I let her go. "Keep me company while I bathe." I take her hand and lead her to the spa room. She watches me as I undress quickly and haul myself in the bath.

"You look tired," she notices.

I sigh as I let my head relax against the bath pillow, enjoying the feel of the hot aromatic water surrounding me. "I just got back from China an hour ago," I say a little hoarsely.

"You must be jet lagged." She comes over and kneels by the edge of the bath, holding her hands out. "May I?" she asks permission.

I grant it. "Do anything you want, Viva."

She reaches out and places a hand to either side of my temples, starting a gentle massage. I close my eyes and let her touch soothe me. It's practically instantaneous, the effect she has on me. The towering headache dissipates, replaced by a feeling of comforting warmth, as if I've been transported back to my mother's womb. How the fuck does she do this? I could almost swear sometimes that she's a witch, putting a magic spell on me. How else to explain this thing she does with just the touch of her hands?

After a while, she gets back on her feet and goes to sit across from me on the chair. I open my eyes and murmur, "Thanks."

"No problem," she smiles.

"Tell me how you've been these last two days."

"Good," she says, "nothing new to report."

"How's Joe's arm?"

"Another week and the cast comes off."

"I bet he can't wait."

"He can't! It was something new and exciting at first, but now all he can do is complain about it."

"Poor little man... Did the cops ever catch the person that did this to him?"

Her expression sours. "They're working on it. At least that's what they say."

"Leave it with me; I'll sort it."

"What, you gonna be my knight in shining armor and save the day?" she queries with a raised brow.

"I want to take care of you and Joe."

Her lips curl. "Thanks, but we can take care of ourselves."

"So, you're happy for the person who did this to get away with it?"

"No, of course not!" she huffs. "Listen, I'm not interested in any kind of vigilante retribution. All I want is to see justice done."

"Then leave it with me."

She sighs. "I get that you're all rich and powerful, Tobias, but I don't like to see that power imbalance between us. You just click your fingers and say, 'Leave it with me'. One of these days, I can imagine you clicking your fingers again, only this time to get rid of the tiresome woman you've been seeing." She clicks hers to demonstrate. "Ta da, gone!"

"You think I can dismiss you from my life just like that?"

"I know you can," she's quick to respond.

"Oh, Viva."

But she's not done. I've somehow opened the floodgates with my "leave it with me" comment, and she's letting loose with what's on her mind. "You know, all this talk we had about you needing to be on your guard in case I'm a fortune hunter. It pisses me off that you think all the risk in this relationship is on you. Bullshit! I have just as much if not more to lose. I'm a little ant you can crush with your shoes whenever you feel like it. Even this very minute as I'm arguing with you, a voice in the back of my head is saying, careful now, or you might lose this lucrative client, lose your job. How are you going to pay rent? What about Joe's soccer practice? The football boots he needs? Am I crazy that I'd jeopardize all of that for an admittedly gorgeous man who fucks like a god? What the—"

I stop her speech, interesting as it is, by the expedient method of hauling her into my arms. I don't care that I'm getting her all wet. I just need to hold her. I trap her face against my chest and kiss the top of her head. "Shh," I tell her. I can feel her tremble in after-reaction to what she's said. "It's alright. We'll figure this out." I stroke her back, gentling her. Eventually, she sags against me, all the fight gone out of her. "So, you missed me, huh?" I whisper into her ear.

She pulls away. "That's what you have to say?"

"Oh, I've lots to say, but we'll start there."

She traces a finger along my chest. "Maybe I missed you a little."

"I missed you a hell of a lot more than a little."

She nods. "That's good."

"You think?"

She shrugs, her gaze fixed on my chest. Oh no, I'm not having her go all meek on me now. "Viva," I bark. "Look at me."

She raises her head reluctantly.

"Viva, I can't tell you what's going to happen between us, how long we'll be together or whether we'll go the distance, but I can tell you this. Your job, your home and your income will be safe. I guarantee it. Now will you take that worry out of the equation and just focus on enjoying what we have?"

"I'll try." She steps back and looks down at her wet clothes in dismay.

I grin. "Looks like you're going to have to take these off and let them dry while you give me a sensual healing massage."

She hesitates, clearly torn over the ethics of doing her job unclothed. "Okay, but I'll keep my panties and bra on, and no touching from you, got it?"

I give her a salute and stroll over to the massage bed, settling myself on it face down. I hear the rustle of clothes as she takes her pants and tunic off, placing them by the radiator to dry. When she's standing beside me again, I raise myself on my elbows and twist to face her. "And one more thing, Viva. If ever you decide you no longer want to see me, *you* will be the one crushing me like an ant." Without waiting for an answer, I lie back down. After a moment, I feel her drizzling warm oil on my back, then her hands gliding over my body. I smile, anticipating an hour of her sensually healing touch.

Chapter 14

Viva

You will be the one crushing me like an ant. I replay Tobias's words in my head as my hands make their journey over his body. Could it be I have as much power over him as he has on me? It's a novel thought.

I know this thing between us is definitely two-sided. That much was made clear last Tuesday. He'd said he was crazy about me, that he fell for me from the moment we met, that he hasn't been with anyone else in two years. It's safe to say the man has caught feelings—as have I. It's almost enough to make me lay down my defences. I've seen past the public face that Tobias presents. He may be photographed at the biggest events with the best known celebrities. He may travel the world brokering business deals and have access to the most powerful leaders. Behind that façade is a lonely man.

Instinctively from the first time I met him, I sensed he craved love, and that his was a generous, loving spirit in return. For two years, every Friday, through the power of my touch, I've lavished my love on him in a way I've never done with any other client. I've taken comfort and joy in seeing how it healed something within him. If I'm honest with myself, I wasn't surprised that he kept coming back to me every week. Deep down, I've known for a long time that he needs me as much as I need him. Because let's face it, I'm lonely too. And somehow through that physical and emotional connection we share each week, he's fed something in my own soul.

But still, I have to be careful, for Joe's sake. Despite my apparent insouciance when Mom was voicing her concerns the other day, I know I have to protect my son from whatever this is. If it were to become common knowledge that I'm dating Tobias, it would have repercussions on Joe. I only have to look at how Tobias has to travel about with bodyguards to know I need to protect my son from that sort of exposure. For now at least, this relationship cannot be allowed to be anything more than what we've agreed.

"Stop overthinking." Tobias's voice takes me unawares.

"Excuse me?"

Slowly, he turns his body around to lie on his back. He fixes me with his gaze. "I can feel it, like jammed electrical signals. You're stressing out in your head."

"You can feel it?"

He smiles lazily. "Yeah. I'm not receiving the full flow of loving energy I usually get. It's like it's being interrupted."

"Seriously, you can feel it?" I've always believed in the healing power of my positive energy, of course. I just didn't think it was quite so obvious.

He takes my hand and holds it to his chest. "I feel it, and I also know how you think. You're going over every word we said, aren't you? You're worrying about this thing between us."

"Do you blame me?"

He releases my hand. "No, I get it. Let me share with you though something I've learned over the years in my line of work. Worry about the things you can have impact over and the stuff out of your control let go."

I pour oil over his chest and begin to massage it in. "Your meaning being?"

"Just that we've fallen for each other. That's done and dusted, out of our control. Think of it as fate. Now all we have to decide is what we're going to do about it, and we're agreed on the parameters, aren't we? Whenever we feel those parameters need changing, we'll talk again."

I circle his nipples with my thumbs. "You make it sound easy."

He sighs in pleasure at the feel of my hands on him. "That bit of it is. The hard part is the days when I can't see you. Then I become Mr Grumpy, according to my assistant." He falls silent, enjoying my sensual touch. I can see his cock is definitely interested. His eyes flutter open. "Are we getting down to business or are you going to tease me again?"

My smile is smug. "I think you know the answer to that, Mr Moore."

He lets out a long breath. "Then do your worst, Viva. Give me the full on, bells and whistle service I pay good money for."

"Oh, I will. Expect nothing less." With that, I set my worries aside and focus on giving Tobias the most blissful experience he's ever had.

Afterwards, I lay a blanket on him and prepare to leave. He stays me with his hand. "Thanks, Viva. That was... more than amazing. I can't think of a better word. You got plans for the weekend?"

"Nothing much. Joe has an invite to his friend's birthday party on Saturday."

"Can I call you in the evening? Maybe we can watch another movie together."

"You got any other exclusives?"

"You bet I have."

I shake my head. "Or maybe we can just watch a classic from the 21st century."

"Whatever you want."

"Okay," I say. "I'd like that."

"Good. Now kiss me goodbye."

I bend down and brush his lips with mine. "Bye, Tobias," I whisper. "Until next week."

☆ ☆ ☆

SATURDAY EVENING, HE calls at nine o'clock. "Joe asleep?" he asks.

"Like a light."

"How was the party?"

I settle myself back on my malleable armchair and answer, "Joe had fun, and I got to catch up with some of the other moms."

"How very momsie of you," he teases.

"Having a kid creates a kind of bond between yourself and others that have gone through something similar," I say in defence. "You know—the trials, the hardships, as well as the proud moments. There was one other mom there who was single like me, so we gravitated towards each other and had a good time talking."

"Hey, I'm not knocking it. I'm glad you found someone to talk to. I can only imagine how transformative an experience having a kid must be."

I stretch out my arms and let the armchair adjust itself around me. "Well, I can say hands on heart it changed my life."

He looks at me speculatively. "I know it hasn't always been easy, but if you could go back, would you have it any different?"

I think about it for a moment. "The one thing I regret, for Joe's sake, is that his father is not involved in his life. I wish that was different, but as to my getting pregnant accidentally, no. I can't imagine life without Joe in it."

"His dad never wanted to be involved?"

"He walked out on us literally a minute after I told him. Next I heard, his lawyers were asking me to sign documents waiving his rights."

"Asshole!" Tobias looks genuinely furious.

"Yeah, he is, but he gifted me Joe, so I can't be too mad at him."

He narrows his eyes. "Just out of interest, how did you manage to get accidentally pregnant? I thought that kind of thing was in the past."

I laugh. "You know when they say a drug is ninety-nine point nine per cent effective? I just happened to fall into that point one category that wasn't. Of course, Dan wouldn't believe it and accused me of getting pregnant on purpose."

"You had the NoPreg implant?"

"Yep."

He leans his face on his hand thoughtfully. "I wonder if you have a legal case against the company that manufactures it."

"Nah. I did check, but apparently that statement on the label covers them for this eventuality."

"I'll let my lawyers look into it," he says decisively.

"Another case of 'leave it with me'?" I ask mockingly.

"Why won't you just let me take care of it?" He sounds annoyed.

"We've talked about this."

"Yes, and I've addressed your concerns. It's no trouble for me to do this, so let me. It's not going to change the dynamics between us."

"Okay," I huff.

"Okay." After a moment, something else occurs to him. "So, when you say you're not going to fall accidentally pregnant again, what do you mean by that?"

"Worried, Mr Moore?"

"Not in the slightest, Ms Parker. Just interested in your strategy."

I shrug. "I have the NoPreg implant, but I supplement it with a good old-fashioned IUD."

"What's that?" he asks with a frown.

"It's an intra-uterine device inserted into my womb to stop implantation. So, double the protection."

"Is it safe?"

"Relax, it's been used effectively for many decades."

"Okay."

I can read his mind like a book. "You're going to look it up, aren't you?"

"Of course."

I laugh. "Oh, Tobias. You are priceless."

"When something matters to me, I'm thorough about it."

"Suit yourself. All I'll say is that it's a safe and effective method of contraception. It doesn't get used much anymore because NoPreg has taken over the market, that's all."

"And I'm sure you'll not mind my checking it out."

I cock my head consideringly. "You know, Tobias, you are a very controlling person."

"How else do you think I've gotten where I am, Viva? You don't get to the top by letting things slide," he says derisively.

I decide it's time to change subject. "Are we going to keep arguing all night?" I ask, a challenge in my voice.

His eyes flare. "I had other things in mind for tonight."

"A movie?"

"Or maybe something else."

I bite my lip, staring at him. "Like what?" I ask, playing dumb.

His voice drops an octave. "Take me to your bedroom, Viva."

In half a moment, I come to a decision. Picking up my communicator from its holder, I walk to my room, taking Tobias—remotely—with me. He glances around at what he can see of it from his device. "This place is very you," he says.

I sit on the edge of my bed. "Now what?"

"Is it in your bedside drawer, Viva? Take out my little gift."

Okay, so we are going there. I withdraw the sex toy from my drawer and hold it out for him to see. "Do you have lube?" Again, I rummage in my drawer and take out a dispenser. "Good," he says, looking satisfied. "Now take off your clothes for me. Do it nice and slow."

He wants a show? I can give him one. I position the communicator holder so it's suspended above the bed, affording him a good view of the proceedings. "You putting me on projection mode?" I ask. It's a function, recently added to the universal program that runs most communicators—designed by Tobias's company of course—where the person on your screen can be projected as a hologram in front of you, looking almost as real as if they were there in person.

"You bet," he drawls.

"Is this striptease going to be a two-way show?" I enquire innocently.

His smile is sinful. "Baby, if you want it to be, all you need to do is ask."

"I want," I say as I tap my own communicator to put him on projection mode. It takes a few moments for his form to fully materialize, but now in front of me I see him on his bed in 3-D. I can almost believe the end wall of my room has magically opened up into his bedroom. My skin breaks out in goosepimples. "Wow," I breathe. "I still can't get used to this."

"It's been a game-changer for me in my business. Sometimes, virtual meetings just don't cut it. You have to be in the room to really see a person and their reactions, but this feels so real that I don't have to travel half as much as I used to."

"It feels so amazingly real, like I could just lean forward and touch you."

His voice is husky as he murmurs, "I know." Then, he gets down to business. "Alright, tit-for-tat. You take off your top then I'll take off my shirt. Nice and slow, remember."

"Yes, sir." I'm wearing an old college T-shirt that I like to sleep in, together with casual lounge pants. It's hardly a sexy outfit, but I try to give the man sitting across from me a decent show. I push the hem up slowly to reveal my belly button and a hint of my bra, then let it drop down again.

"Tease," he mutters.

"All in good time, baby." There's a definite tent in the groin of his pants. Empowered, I glide my hands down my body, palming my breasts through the fabric of the T-shirt, until I get to the hem again. I slide it up slowly, one inch at a time, taking it all the way off and throwing it across the bed. I face him. "Now, your turn. Nice and slow."

With a smirk, he kneels on his bed and, mimicking my earlier actions, plays with the hem of his shirt, teasing me with a glimpse of his happy trail. My eyes narrow. Okay, not funny. I want to see it all. "Alright, asshole. Not so slow," I grumble.

He drops the hem. "What, you don't want a show?"

"Will you take that off already?" I demand, my patience at an end.

"Here's the thing," he says, keeping me waiting. "You're still wearing a bra, while under this shirt, there's nada. Doesn't seem fair somehow."

My hands are already at the front clasp of my bra. I shed the offending garment and, quid pro quo, he pulls off that damned shirt, baring his beautiful chest. Oh God! This doesn't get old. No one has the right to look this good.

He runs his hands over himself, pinching his nipples much as I would if I were touching him. His eyes are glued to me. "Touch yourself, Viva."

I cup my breasts, holding them up as if in offering to him. He groans, "So pretty." Then it's my turn to play with my nipples, making them stand nice and firm. He growls, "So fucking pretty." He brings his hungry eyes back up to my face. "No more games, Viva. Get naked, now." With one downward pull, he removes his pants and briefs, letting me see him in his full glory. I'm quick to reciprocate. No surprise my panties are already wet with my desire. "Part your legs; let me see you touch your pussy," grits Tobias. I do as he says, putting my fingers to my clit, while in front of me, I see him pull on his engorged cock.

I'm close, but he won't let me come just yet. Instead, he points with his head towards the replica of his cock that sits by my side. "Set it up," he instructs, "and attach my cock to it." It's a simple matter to do it, and within seconds, the sex toy is ready to use. Across from me, I see him hold up a replica device to the one I have. "I have the controls right here," he says, looking pleased with himself. "Now this is what I want you to do. First, lube up my cock. I can see how wet you are, but I want to fuck you hard tonight." I do as instructed, feeling my excitement levels rise. "Good girl. Now get on your hands and knees, facing away from me. Position my cock on your pussy."

With a slight shiver, I turn to face the headboard, placing the sex contraption behind me. It takes a few efforts before I get the dildo cock to my entrance. "That's it, baby," he croons. "You're so ready for me. I'm going to enter you now. You don't need to do anything more; just feel." Slowly, his long, thick cock pushes all the way inside me. Damn if it doesn't feel like the real thing. "Feel my cock, Viva!"

"I do. Feels good," I moan.

He pulls back a little, then plunges into me again. "Just look at you, taking my cock so well." He begins to move in a circular motion inside me, finding my G-spot and creating delicious friction. Yet another thing this clever toy can do. I'd bet anything his company had something to do with the making of it. As if he reads my mind, he informs me, "We're still in the prototype phase, but this one is a special edition made uniquely for me, and you." His cock begins to thrust faster and deeper. His voice is husky and low behind me, "That's right, baby. You can take it."

A moment later, something brushes along my clit in a fluttering motion. Goddamn. At this rate, I'm not going to last. "Come for me, Viva," he demands. "I want your first orgasm now." *There's going to be more than one?* The thought escapes my mind as I'm rocked by a wave of delicious sensation.

"Ah," I moan as my climax reaches its completion.

He stills, lodged deep inside me. The fluttering on my clit also ceases. I take a deep calming breath. "Good girl," he purrs. "Pull up that pillow and rest your head on it. We're going to be here for quite a while. How do you feel?"

"Good," I sigh, relaxing onto the pillow, elbows down by my side.

"One of the advantages of fucking you like this," he says conversationally, "is that I can go on and on until I think you've had enough." His tone changes. "Get ready, Viva, for round two." He's barely finished speaking before he's fucking me again, in long, deep, slow strokes. This second time around, he's in no rush. He takes his time, varying the angle and strokes of his clever cock. In between, he showers me with words of praise, telling me how beautiful I look and what a good girl I am. I never realized until now that my kink was praise. Before I know it, I'm experiencing a sweet, gentle orgasm, a light pulsing of my internal walls.

I turn my head around to see him. His gray eyes are almost the color of slate, dark with lust. He lets his cock rest inside me, never taking it out. His actual cock is rock hard, the purple tip dripping with precum. "One more round," he says in a rasping voice. "Brace yourself, Viva. Now's time for the hardest fuck of all." And so, he begins.

Right from the start, his thrusts are hard and fast. He pounds into me, grunting words of lust and encouragement. "That's it. Take me. You can do it. Good girl. Ah. Yes. Fucking take it." Somewhere along the line, he activates the fluttering motion on my clit. He turns it up to the highest vibration setting. I cry out loud. I don't know how much more of this I can take. But that's not all. There's something wet easing its way into my back hole and pulsing into me. Oh fuck.

"You gonna come for me?" he demands.

"Ah!" I moan.

"I said come for me!"

My orgasm detonates sending me into crazy convulsions. All I can do is moan endlessly with each sublime clench of my pussy. When it's over, I collapse in a daze, unable to move. I feel him gently withdraw the sex toy from me. His voice is calm and soothing. "That was beautiful, Viva, so beautiful. When you're ready, baby, get yourself up and start a hot bath. I wish I could do it for you, but I can't."

I gather my strength to turn around on the bed. He's sitting across from me, his chest covered in pearly cum. "You came too," I murmur hoarsely.

"Goddamn right I did. That was the hottest thing I've ever seen."

I smile wanly.

"You got some bath salts for your sorely used pussy?"

"I do. Not the ones from Sensual Healing—they're kinda out of my price range—but I have my own home-made concoction."

He nods gravely. "They'll have to do for tonight. I'll make sure to send you a case of Sensual Healing salts."

"Tobias! I wasn't asking for some."

"But you're getting them nonetheless. Now don't argue. Just go run that bath."

I sigh. "Okay. You coming with me?"

He raises a brow. "What do you think?"

I tap my communicator to end projection mode and pick it up. In the bathroom, I quickly tap the button for a full hot bath, then take out the jar of home-made aromatic salts. I pour a handful into the water, noticing that Tobias is likewise engaged in his own bathroom. I place my communicator in its holder across from me, and on a whim, tap the projection function again. By the time I've settled myself in, Tobias has materialized in front of me, his head resting against the edge of his bath, water lapping at his chest. "This is so fucking cool," I say. "It's as if you're in the bath with me."

"It's fucking great," he concurs.

I give a luxurious stretch of my legs in the water, letting it lap at my sore pussy. Which reminds me. "That sex toy prototype. Does it have a name yet?"

"I'm thinking of calling it Viva's fantasy."

I snort. "Don't you even dare." I pause, then go on, "But I can tell you this. When it comes to the market, it's going to sell like hotcakes, maybe double your fortune."

"You liked it that much?"

I huff, not deigning to answer.

After a while, he says, "So, I've been thinking, Viva. I want to make an addendum to our agreement."

I eye him warily. "What kind of addendum?"

"I see you twice a week in person, once at my home and once at Sensual Healing, but in addition to that, I want two evenings a week of your virtual time—after Joe has gone to bed."

I want to play hardball, I really do, but honestly? I can't say no to that. "Fine," is all I can come up with.

"Good girl," he rumbles in satisfaction.

Chapter 15

Tobias

Six weeks later

"Good news," says Ralph, breezing into my office. I'm lounging on a malleable armchair in my thinking nook. This is where I do my deep thinking and where I come up with solutions to seemingly intractable problems. I pause my musings to look up at my assistant. He knows better than to disturb me, unless it's for something important.

"Troy has been accepted on the Venorian exchange program."

"That's hardly news, Ralph," I say with a frown. "It was a foregone conclusion."

"Ah, but that's not the good news I wanted to share. The person he's trading places with? None other than a Venorian named Pravol who is a leading commander in their space fleet. He was the one who made first contact with Ambassador Garcia last year, remember? And that's not all. Another of the aliens on the exchange, a guy named Shuban, just happens to be a leading aeronautics engineer specializing in spaceship design."

I stare at Ralph. "Fucking genius," I say. "We need to make sure this guy, Shuban, is on board to work with us as well as Pravol. Who's he exchanging places with?"

Ralph glances at his communicator. "Some doctor named Diego Sanchez who works in genetic research."

"We need to make sure Shuban is seconded to us—there's no point in him working at a medical research center during his six months here."

Ralph nods. "I'll work on it." He pauses. "There's one more thing."

"Spit it out, Ralph."

"There's a big reception being held in honor of the visiting Venorians when they arrive on the Mars colony. Ambassador Garcia has sent you a personal invite."

"Fine. I'd like to get a first look at them when they arrive. Make the arrangements."

Ralph purses his lips. "It's this Friday."

Damn. No way am I missing my Friday session with Viva. But holy hell, I need to be at that reception. I come to a quick decision. "Make arrangements for Viva to accompany me, discreetly, as my massage therapist. And get her an invite to the reception as well."

"You got it."

I speak to my communicator. "Athena, message for Viva... Baby, are you busy? I need to speak to you... Athena send message."

Hardly a minute passes before Viva calls me back. "Hey babe, what's up?" Her face wears a worried expression.

"Nothing to worry about. I have a proposition for you, Viva. I'm going to need to be out of town this Friday, but I'm sure as heck not missing my sensual healing treatment. So, the only way around it is for you to travel with me. I'll pay all your expenses of course, including any losses from appointments you have to cancel."

She bites her lip in concentration. "How long would I need to be away?"

"Can you manage two nights away from Joe?"

She sighs. "I guess. Where are we going?"

"Only to Mars," I say breezily.

Her eyes nearly bulge. "What the fuck?"

"I said Mars. Have you ever travelled in space?"

"Never."

"Well, now's your chance. Plus, you'll get to meet some visiting aliens. You'll be one of the first to say hi to the Venorians. How does that sound?"

She's staring at me as if I've grown two heads. "For real? You're not kidding me?"

"Absolutely for real."

"Shit. I don't know what to say."

"Just say yes."

She smiles dazedly. "Yes. I never expected, never dreamed I would go into space. That kind of thing is way out of my price bracket."

I feel a tug somewhere in the region of my chest. If I have anything to do with it, from now on she'll go wherever she dreams, no matter the price. Briskly, I say, "We'll leave very early Thursday, which should get us to Mars the following morning. That will give us time to rest, enjoy a sensual healing treatment, then go attend the reception and fly back to Earth straight after, so we can return by Saturday evening."

She thinks it over. "I'll have to make it up to Joe. Forgive me, Tobias, but in that case, I won't be able to come to you tonight."

I swallow my disappointment. "That's fair."

"I have to go get ready for my next client."

"Yeah. I'll call you tonight."

"Okay."

I end the call and go back to the problem I was mulling over before Ralph barged in on me. How to get Viva to live with me openly as my partner. There's no doubt in my mind that I want to be with her, and that she wants to be with me. I know the main obstacle is the high profile life I lead, and the effect it would have on Joe. She sees how I live, surrounded by bodyguards, and she doesn't want that for him. That's understandable. Normality is not what you get when you become part of my family. I know from experience, though, that all intractable problems have a solution. I simply have to find it.

Chapter 16

Viva

Riding the super-subway on my way home, all I can think about is this trip to Mars, not to mention the fact I'll be spending two nights and three days with Tobias—or at least I assume so. Maybe I'm wrong. I've never been on a spaceship before. Will we even sit together? Our relationship is not public, so I guess we probably won't. I'll be the secret lover tucked away discreetly in the corner. I grimace at the thought.

These past few weeks have been quite a whirlwind. Although we only see each other in person twice a week, we talk every day, spending hours together on our communicators in the evenings, unless Tobias has some business event to attend, and even then, he finds the time to call me. We're acting all loved up, snatching every possible stolen moment to be together. Well, why not? We are, after all, in love. I see what this is with him and me. We haven't declared our love, at least not in so many words. It's more a case of "I'm crazy about you" or "I need you so much", but it all equates to the same thing. And sometimes, you don't need words. You can just feel it.

Which makes the nature of our secret relationship all the more problematic. Joe has spoken to Tobias several times now, though they have never met in person. There's a strict separation between my home life and my life with Tobias. Is that sustainable? Is it even desirable? Shouldn't we be opening ourselves up gradually to the idea of making our relationship a real one where we can publicly be together? Does Tobias even want that? We haven't had any further talks about changing the "parameters".

And then there's the problem of his high profile as the richest man in the world. I've been stalking him secretly on social media, and I see the many stories written and conjectures made about him. I see how he's hounded by reporters wherever he goes. I see the glitzy parties he attends. The life he leads is not for me, or for Joe. I can't see how that can change. So, perhaps we're doomed to being perpetual secret lovers, never out in the open.

I get home in time to change and then collect Joe from school. It's only a few blocks away, so we walk the journey home. "Joe," I broach the subject. "Remember my friend Tobias?"

"Yeah. He's my friend too. He told me so."

I laugh. "Well, my friend and yours, Tobias, is going on a special journey and he has asked me to go with him. You know that as well as being my friend, he is also someone I work with. So, I'll be going with him to do some work and earning money, but it means I'll have to be gone a few days."

His mouth turns down. "Why can't I come too?"

I sigh. "If this were a vacation and you didn't have school, then maybe you could. But I'm going for work, sweet boy. I wouldn't be able to take care of you while I worked. So on Thursday, you'll be going to stay with Grandma for two sleeps, and then I'll be back on Saturday."

"I don't want to," he says sulkily.

"What, you don't want to bake cookies with Grandma? Or have Ben come over and play Koondles with you?"

"I do!"

"Well then, you do want to go to Grandma's."

"But I don't want you to go, Momma."

"Oh honey, I'll be back before you know it. When you're having fun, time goes by so quickly. And you know, I might come back with a special something for you." Perhaps it's not the best idea to bribe him with a gift, but I'm low on options right now.

He looks ever so slightly interested. "What kind of something?"

"It'll be a surprise." I'm banking on the fact the tourist shops on Mars must have something to excite my son.

I leave it at that. As with most children, Joe has the ability to be in the moment, and Thursday is too far away to be of much more concern. That night, when I put him to bed, I relent and read him two of his favorite stories. Then, I kiss his downy cheek and bid him goodnight.

Later, Tobias calls. I tell him about my conversation with Joe, feeling a pang of guilt about what I'm proposing to do. I have never left my son longer than overnight. He listens quietly. Finally, he says, "I know it's going to be a wrench leaving him for two nights, Viva. There's nothing I can say to change that. But he'll be in a safe and familiar environment with your mom, and I bet he'll have a good time after he gets over the initial bout of tears. I'm not going to apologize for taking you with me. I want you to have this experience."

"I want it too."

"We'll buy him something very special on Mars."

"Yeah, I hope we find something for him. I have no idea what the shops are like on the colony."

He smirks. "Leave it with me, Viva."

I simply shake my head, not bothering to argue. Then I ask him about the journey. "What will it be like on the spaceship?"

"You'll have to brace yourself for the take-off, but after that, it's plain sailing, I promise. It'll take us around twenty-four hours to get there, so it's a long journey. Some of that time, we can use the sleep pods. For the rest, there's the usual range of onscreen entertainment."

"Will I have to sit apart from you."

He sighs. "I'm afraid so, Viva. It would invite unwelcome attention if we sat together. But I'll make sure you have a comfortable seat and I'll get Ralph to sit with you so you're not alone. He's tolerable company."

Tobias has spoken of Ralph a time or two, so I know he's his assistant and close confidant. "Okay," I murmur.

"When it's time for sleep, I'll get Ralph to discreetly bring you to my pod. We'll sleep together," he says decisively.

"That's good."

"Viva."

"Yes?"

"Get naked, now. I need to fuck you."

MARS IS BOTH what I expected and different. The landscape outside, from my brief view as our ship docks at the station, is dry and arid, much like the pictures I've seen of it. But there is something curiously majestic about the endless vista of red earth and rocky dunes.

The journey here was uneventful, though long. Take-off from Earth was indeed a bracing experience—not something I'll wish to repeat in a hurry. As we hurled through the atmosphere at God knows how many miles per hour, I prayed, and prayed. And prayed again. Maybe this is my way to rediscover religion.

Now I'm here though, it all seems worth it. Inside the massive complex, mainly built of course by Tobias's company, is a bustling city comprising a main thoroughfare with shops and restaurants, from where corridors lead to different residential and working sectors. On arrival from afar, I saw Tobias being greeted by Ambassador Garcia, the leader of this colony, and whisked away for some meetings. Ralph too has gone with them, but not before he ensured I was put in the capable hands of Dana, one of the colony hosts, who escorted me to the quarters where I'll be staying.

I walk through these now, investigating. There's a functional en-suite bedroom, a small work and entertainment zone, and a kitchenette with a supply of dehydrated food pods and a top-of-the-range CuisiPod. Feeling hungry, I riffle through the pods and choose a grilled cheese sandwich, then drop it into the CuisiPod and press the start button. While that cooks, I explore further. There's a door along the entrance corridor which I tap open. On the other side is a fully set-up treatment room, with a massage bed, towels and scented candles. Aha, my place of work while here on Mars. I notice another door on the other side of that room. On tapping it, I enter a much bigger, luxuriously appointed suite of rooms. No guessing who will be staying here.

Explorations over, I return to my own more modest room and take out my cheese sandwich. I grab another pod, this time to brew me a cup of coffee. Perching on a stool at the small breakfast bar, I wolf down my food while taking out my communicator to message Mom and let her know I've arrived safe and well. She responds, telling me Joe is having a good time at his grandma's. That helps put my mind at rest. As I go to put my communicator down, I get a call from Tobias.

"Hey."

"Viva. You good?"

"Sure."

He sighs. "Sorry, I couldn't be with you. Looks like I'm going to be busy for at least another two hours. You got everything you need?"

"Yeah, it's all good. I think I might go explore the sights."

"You do that. I've made sure the colony host is available to you. Just page them any time you want to go out. Oh and Viva, anything you buy, put it on my tab."

I raise my brows. "You know I won't."

"If you don't, I'll simply make my tip for today's massage even more generous than usual. Get Joe something special from me, please."

"Hmm. We'll see. Will you want your treatment as soon as you get back?"

His eyes flare a bright gray. "Yes, please. If you don't mind. Then we can rest together before getting ready for the reception."

"Okay, that works for me."

His smile is warm. "See you soon, Viva. Go in peace."

"Go in peace, Tobias."

I spend the next hour and a half exploring the sights, escorted by Dana, the colony host. He takes me to the observatory, where I'm able to immerse myself in more of the Martian landscape, then on to the gift shops on the main thoroughfare. I browse through the overpriced touristy wares, which seeing as we're only two weeks away from Valentine's Day, are full of pink hearts and stuff that's really not for me. I shake my head in disgust. I hate the way the pure act of falling in love is commercially exploited like this. To be fair, I've never been a fan of this supposed romantic day. What good are the heart-shaped cookies and red roses when the guy giving them to you ups and leaves a week later? After a good look through all the shops, I finally decide on a Mars-themed Koondles set for Joe and a pretty necklace for Mom made from delicately carved Martian rocks. As I try to pay for them with my communicator, I'm told by the checkout bot that all my purchases have already been charged to Mr Moore's account. Cheeky bastard.

Then I'm back in my quarters, getting changed into my Sensual Healing pants and tunic, and getting everything ready for Tobias's treatment. This is work, I remind myself, and even though I'm not in my usual environment, I need to ensure Tobias gets as fulfilling a treatment as he would otherwise. In his luxurious suite, I run a hot spa bath and drop Sensual Healing salts into it. A sound behind me has me look around. Tobias stands in the doorway of the bathroom, hooded eyes regarding me like a hawk.

"Good afternoon, Mr Moore," I say, getting into professional mode. "Your bath is ready."

He quirks his lips at the formality of my speech and strolls forward, beginning to undress. Coming to a stop before me, he removes his unbuttoned shirt and throws it carelessly to the floor. His pants and briefs are next. Then, beautifully naked, he stands and lets me ogle him for one brief moment before getting into the steaming bath.

"Ah," he sighs. "That's good."

"Did your meetings go well?" I ask.

"As well as is to be expected. We're one little step closer to making those third generation spaceships a reality."

"Do you really think your new ships will be fast enough to travel to Ven and other planets in that quadrant?" I wonder curiously.

His eyes harden with determination. "I do. It won't be easy, and there'll be hiccups along the way, but we'll get there." I can sense this project means a lot to him. And rightly so. With that kind of technology, humanity could travel much farther than we have ever done before, discovering new alien civilizations.

We talk a few minutes more. There's something easy and comfortable about how we are together—the result of our greater intimacy, no doubt. It's not something I've had in any previous relationship though. This thing with Tobias is way different. My heart squeezes in my chest. Funny how it is my body that knew I loved him well before my mind did.

Tobias sits up in the bath and scorches me with his stare. "If you keep looking at me like that, Viva, I'm going to drag you straight to bed," he growls.

I stand, rubbing my damp palms on the fabric of my pants. "Then I guess we better get started on your treatment," I reply shakily. I grab hold of a towel and offer it to him. Slowly, like a predator about to leap on its prey, he stands and steps out of the bath, taking the towel from me. His eyes never leave me as he dries his body. When he's done, he throws it carelessly aside.

"Come here, Viva," he says softly.

"We're supposed to keep things professional for your treatments," I hedge.

"Viva."

"You know it makes it harder to take your money if I'm not doing honest work in return. I'm not your kept woman."

"I know. Come here, Viva, please."

I take a step closer to him. Then another. His hands bury themselves in my hair. "We'll get to the treatment in a minute," he whispers. "But first, I need this." And then he kisses me.

We eventually make it to the massage room, and I manage to give Tobias a decent enough treatment. Afterwards, he takes me to bed. We make love, then sleep, then make love again. We must have fallen into another light doze, because I'm brought awake again by Athena's voice telling us it's six pm local time. Beside me, Tobias stretches lazily. "Time to get up, beautiful," he tells me in a gravelly voice.

I force myself to wake, battling the fog of spaceship lag. With a loud yawn, I get out bed, watched by him. "See you in a while," I mumble and head back to my own room where I left my clothes bag. For this reception, I packed my fanciest dress, a deep blue shimmery affair that shows off my toned legs. I get ready quickly, fixing my hair into a loose knot with a few artful strands framing my face. I don't bother with too much make up. Just a light dusting of face powder and a little eye definition. For my lips, a coat of blush pink gloss. Lastly, I affix a pair of stud earrings and slip my feet into invisible wedge heels. I twirl in front of the mirror, examining myself from all angles. I'll do.

When I rejoin Tobias, I find him in conversation with Ralph, attired in superbly-cut formalwear. Their talk ceases as they catch sight of me, the both of them staring for a moment too long.

I glance down at myself. "What is it? Am I not dressed smart enough?"

"Fuck," mutters Tobias.

Ralph clears his throat. "What he means is that you look beautiful, Viva."

Tobias throws his assistant an irritated glance. "Shut up, Ralph," he says and comes towards me. "But he's right. You look beautiful, Viva."

I let out a breath in relief. "Thanks."

There's a buzzing sound at the door. One of his bodyguards checks it and gives him a nod. Tobias addresses me with a frown. "That's my ride. Viva baby, we can't be seen arriving together, not without occasioning the kind of gossip we really don't want. Ralph will escort you to the reception, and he'll stay with you the whole time." That last is said with a pointed look at Ralph who nods in confirmation. Poor guy, having to play nursemaid to me when he's probably got a ton more interesting things to do.

Turning back to me, Tobias touches a finger to my cheek gently. Speaking softly so only I can hear, he says, "I wish I could have you on my arm, baby, but we both know why that's not a good idea."

I swallow the lump in my throat. "I understand." And I do, but I can't help the bitter bile that forms when I realize once again how it will be. Me, his hidden secret in the corner while he steps into the limelight. Do I really want this for my life? I try to shake these negative thoughts away as I paste on a smile and say, "Have fun."

"You too. I'll see you here afterwards." With one last frowning glance in my direction, Tobias leaves, followed by his ever present bodyguards.

In the silence that ensues, I see Ralph checking his communicator. Finally, he looks to me, a friendly expression on his face. "Ready to go to the party?"

"Sure. I'm sorry you got roped in to nursemaid me."

His smile grows wider. "I think between Tobias and me, I got the better deal. Come on, let's go."

We arrive at the reception some ten minutes later. Our invitations are checked at the door, then we're in, a passing bot offering us a glass of champagne. The event is being held in a grand looking ballroom with an old world feel to it. The burgundy carpeted floors—vantex of course—offset the cream and gold pattern of the walls, which are decorated with antique looking sconces that cast a soft golden light over the room. The place is already bustling with people, all of them expensively dressed.

I look around for Tobias but don't at first catch sight of him. "Over there," breathes Ralph, pointing with his chin.

I follow the line of his gaze and finally see the man I love. He's standing in a small group with a person I recognize as Ambassador Garcia and a very tall, oddly-dressed man. It takes me a moment to realize that he must be one of the Venorian aliens.

"Is that—"

"Yes, it's Pravol, the Venorian who will be coming to work for us as part of the exchange."

"He's big!"

"Yes. I'd say he's at least six feet seven. But apart from the height, he could almost pass off as human."

"Growing up, I always thought aliens would have horns or tails or something," I say, trying not to stare too hard at this particular alien.

Ralph laughs. "Yes, me too. I guess human imagination got a little too overactive." He touches my arm lightly. "Let's go check out the buffet. I heard they pulled out all the stops and brought in real meat from Earth for this." Deftly, he guides me through the throng of people towards the far corner of the room where I see a long rectangular table heaving with food. With a grin, Ralph procures a plate for me. "Let's load up."

I take a look at the decadent spread, not knowing where to start. I have never seen this level of extravagance before. I look down to what looks like smoked salmon, which I have only tasted once before in my life, on little rounded pancakes. I decide to try one. Next to that are shrimps in a buttery looking sauce, which I also decide to try out. By the time I'm done, the food on my plate is a loaded pyramid of luxurious delicacies. I take comfort in the fact Ralph is being no less of a glutton. He looks at me shamefacedly. "I'll have to do a double workout back on Earth to make up for this."

I laugh. "Yeah, me too. Could you hold my plate for just a minute? I want to take pictures for back home."

"No problem."

As discreetly as possible, I take out my communicator and snatch a quick video, which I send to Mom with the message, "That's how the higher ups eat! Wish I could save some for you." Then, I tuck into my feast. I hardly know anyone at this reception, and I'd much rather eat than stand around looking foolish. Plus, it gives me a good vantage point to people watch. I glance again in Tobias's direction and for a few sizzling seconds, our eyes meet. I make a show of biting into my meat samosa and nodding happily to let him know the food's delicious. He smiles. Then his attention shifts as someone speaks to him.

Ralph has not failed to observe this little byplay. "You're good for him," he muses softly.

"Good for him how?" I ask, genuinely wanting to know.

"In ten years of knowing him, I don't think I've seen Tobias smile half as much as he has this past month."

"I'm glad," I say, then I add, "But it's complicated."

"Worthwhile things usually are," he points out.

"I guess. I just don't see how we're going to work this one out. Look at us tonight, having to stand apart and pretend we're not an item."

"Yeah," he sighs. "That sucks." His attention is diverted when he spots an acquaintance of his and waves him over. The man and his female companion head towards us.

"Ralph, my man, how you doing?"

"I'm being a pig, as you can see," remarks Ralph humorously. He turns to me, making the introductions. "Viva, this is Troy, a colleague of mine who will be going on the Venorian exchange. Troy, meet Viva, who's the reason why Tobias never has meetings at six o'clock on a Friday."

Troy regards me curiously, so I explain, "I'm his massage therapist."

"Ah, got it." Troy smiles, "Nice to meet you, Viva." He looks to the attractive woman beside him. "This is Martha, a friend of mine."

Martha gives a wry smile. "Nice to meet you all. What Troy has kindly omitted to say, is that I was with him on the candidate list for the exchange program, but unfortunately, I didn't get selected."

"More fool them!" exclaims Troy, curling his lips.

Martha shrugs. "But as second prize, I get to attend this glitzy reception and feast on this food. Did you see, they have real fillet mignon?"

Ralph points with his fork to the steak on his plate. "I did."

"Have you met any of the aliens yet?" I ask curiously.

Troy chuckles. "I have. Those big guys are the stuff of wet dreams." He gives an exaggerated sigh.

"Could you introduce us to them?" asks Ralph. "I know Viva is dying to meet one."

"Sure." Troy looks around. "There's Pravol and Treylor. Come with me, and we'll say hi."

I put my plate down on a side table and follow Troy, along with Ralph. He leads us to a small group of people gathered around the tall figure of Pravol. Too late, I notice Tobias standing in that group and frowning at me as I approach. Oblivious to this, Troy walks up to the group, saying in confident tones, "Hi everyone, sorry to interrupt. Pravol, I have some friends here who would love to meet you." He beckons me forward with a friendly smile. "Pravol, this is Viva, and with her is Ralph."

I step forward awkwardly. Pravol nods solemnly then approaches to give the Venorian style of greeting. I've read about this. Apparently, Venorians say hi by touching each other's foreheads. Before I know it, this great big alien has a hand to my cheek and is bringing his forehead to mine.

He's so big and powerful looking. It's a good thing my heart already belongs to Tobias because this guy is lethally sexy. He steps back with a bow and says, "I am honored to meet Tobias's mate. Viva, this is Treylor, who will also soon be my mate." I have very little time to react to these bizarre words before a tall Venorian female steps towards me and greets me in the same way. As she's touching her forehead to mine, my mind is spinning in a panic. *Shit, shit, shit, our secret's out.*

She steps back and bows, saying, "I am honored to meet you, Viva." Then I see her slapping Pravol on his broad chest and whispering something in his ear. To my surprise, his face flushes a darker bronze as he eyes me apologetically.

Troy laughs, unaware of the tension around him. "No, Pravol, you've got the wrong end of the stick. Viva is Tobias's massage therapist, not his mate." He eyes me in amusement. "Mates are the Venorian equivalent of a husband or wife. Maybe he thought you were mated to Tobias because he caught a trace of his scent on you," he says by way of explanation.

I don't know what to say to this. Ralph steps forward and introduces himself to the Venorian couple, diverting the attention from me, but I catch a few speculative looks thrown my way from two other people standing in the group, Ambassador Garcia and a man who looks vaguely familiar, though I can't place where I've seen his face before. I finally get the courage to glance quickly at Tobias, but he's studiously ignoring me. *Great.* A moment later, Ralph takes my arm, saying, "If you'll excuse us, we'll leave you to enjoy the rest of your meal. Apologies for the interruption." Then he's marching me back to where we were before. "Well, that was awkward," he mutters once we're out of earshot.

"Am I in trouble?" I ask worriedly.

He presses his lips together, deep in thought. "Probably not. I don't think Ambassador Garcia is one to gossip, though I can't be sure about Lucas Rivera, the guy standing next to her."

"So that's who he is!" I remember now where I've seen this guy's face before. He's some smarmy politician who was running for a congressional seat in my district. I ponder the matter further. "These aliens are known for their enhanced sense of smell. I suppose it might make sense that he scented Tobias on me after I'd given him a massage. That would explain his comment."

"Yes, it would. Don't worry, Viva, I don't think anyone will make anything of it."

We rejoin Martha and a few other people who also, it turns out, are on the Venorian exchange program. We finish our meal in companiable conversation, and I begin to relax, even to enjoy the occasion. I've just had a delicious meal and met a super sexy alien. Not something that happens every day.

The room goes silent as we hear the clink of a champagne glass. It's Ambassador Garcia, addressing the gathering. "A year ago," she says in a clear, authoritative voice, "I had the honor and privilege to become the first human to make contact with the Venorian people. That fateful day, we took a massive step forward into a greater understanding of the universe around us, perhaps only rivalled by Neil Armstrong's first footsteps on the moon over a century ago. We had no way of knowing if the aliens hailing us were friends or foes, yet we were determined to reach out the hand of friendship. So, it gives me great pleasure to be standing here today, welcoming among us our new friends, the Venorians. Through this exchange program, I believe we will be fostering even greater understanding and cooperation. Welcome, my friends. Let us raise a glass in a toast to our enduring friendship."

We all raise our glasses of champagne, helpfully refilled by the house bots, and give a toast. I glimpse a group of reporters filming this speech and sending their reports to their various media outlets. It occurs to me that Mom will be seeing this footage on the news reports back home. I'm actually witnessing history being made. A sense of excitement and pride comes over me, and all at once, I'm profoundly grateful that Tobias saw fit to bring me here, no matter that I can't be by his side.

I finish up my second glass of champagne and hand it to a passing bot. I rarely drink alcohol, so this is really my limit. Already, I can feel a buzz and a slight dizziness. Ralph excuses himself to go to the bathroom, and I decide to head there too. "I'll come with you," says Martha, and we go together to make use of the facilities. As we emerge from the bathroom, we happen to cross paths with a lone Venorian male. I smile at him politely and say hi. He's a stern looking giant with cool blue eyes and shiny black hair swept back from his brow in some kind of elaborate knot. At my greeting, he approaches, evidently wanting to give me a Venorian-style hello. I let him place a hand to my cheek and his forehead to mine, thinking yet again that it's a good thing my heart belongs to Tobias, else I'd be drooling all evening over these gorgeous Venorians. He steps back and bows. "I am Shuban," he says. "It is an honor to meet Tobias's mate."

Not again! I don't get the chance to correct him as he swiftly turns to Martha and greets her in the same way as me. She steps back from him hurriedly, looking very flustered. His eyes narrow at her. "You sensed me," he says, his tone mildly accusing.

"I-I did," she stammers. "W-was that wrong?"

"No. I am surprised. None of the other humans we have met can read our minds."

"Oh."

He smiles suddenly at her, and his blue eyes twinkle. "You are a beautiful woman. I hope I did not offend."

"Not at all," mumbles Martha. "I'm flattered."

"Perhaps, if you are to return to Earth with us, we can enjoy each other's company."

She nods her head. "Perhaps."

He then leans towards her and whispers something in her ear which makes her flush rosily. A moment later, he's gone, making his way to the bathroom.

I stare at Martha, perplexed. "What was that all about?"

"I think," she says dazedly, "I've just been propositioned by an alien."

"I still don't get it. Why did he say that thing about humans reading minds?"

She lets out a deep, calming breath. "I believe the Venorians have an ability to read minds. That's what they do when they touch foreheads. For some reason, I sensed his thoughts as he read mine."

"So that's why—" I stop myself. Martha doesn't know about Tobias and me. But that would explain why the Venorians keep calling me Tobias's mate. Could it be they read my mind when they touched my forehead? If so, this is massive. Epic. Aliens with telepathic abilities. I need to tell Tobias. "Never mind," I say to Martha. "Let's go find our friends."

We weave our way through the crowds, heading towards where Ralph is standing with Troy and a few other people on the Venorian exchange program. We've nearly reached them when I'm stopped yet again by someone crossing my path. "Well hello there," says Lucas Rivera. "Tobias Moore's massage therapist, or is that his mate?" he asks with an ironic lift of one brow.

"That was just a misunderstanding," I tell him hurriedly. "I gave Mr Moore a treatment earlier today, and

I suppose the Venorians, with their superior sense of smell, picked up his scent on me."

"You must be very good at massage therapy for Tobias to have brought you all the way here with him," continues Lucas Rivera.

I shrug. "I suppose so. I try my best."

"Where is it you practise massage? I would love to experience one of your treatments."

There's no polite way to avoid giving him an answer, despite my sudden reluctance to do so. He's undoubtedly good looking, but there's something distinctly slimy about this politician. I can sense it. Somehow, I'm not sure I would find it in me to summon loving energy for him during a treatment.

Stiffly, I say, "I practise as a master healer at Sensual Healing, though I should warn you there's a long waiting list for my services."

He smiles. "I'm intrigued!" With that, he takes out his communicator and does a search for Sensual Healing, finding the online media pack and perusing it quickly. He reads aloud from the marketing blurb, "Our deeply healing sensual treatment involves intimate touch by our highly trained master healers, resulting in intense bliss and relaxation." He leers up at me. "Does that mean what I think it does?" He chuckles, not waiting for an answer. "Now I know why Tobias insists on bringing you here with him."

I'm proud of the work I do, and I hate how this man cheapens it. My cheeks flush in a mixture of embarrassment and anger. I take a deep breath to stop myself from saying anything foolish. Instead, I go for, "If you will excuse me, my friends are beckoning me." I start moving in their direction, but he stops me with a hand on my arm.

"Not so fast, Viva. Seeing as you're here on Mars, perhaps you might give me a treatment this evening. I'm curious to see what makes them so special, and I'm willing to pay well. Shall we say in an hour?"

I shake my head vehemently. "I'm sorry, Mr Rivera, but that will not be possible."

"Why not? I don't see any other clients clamoring for your time right now. Come on, I'm willing to pay double your usual rate. This reception is nearly over. We could head over to my quarters now."

I speak slowly, wanting to maintain my control and to be crystal clear. "Mr Rivera, I have already said no. I ask you respectfully now to let go of my arm."

He keeps his hand where it is. "Why do you say no? My money's as good as anyone's. Or is there more to your relationship with Tobias than meets the eye? That's it, isn't it?"

"Mr Rivera, please remove your hand from my arm."

A voice behind me speaks in a voice laced with fury. "You heard what the lady said. Take your fucking hand off her now."

Chapter 17

Tobias

This is a historic occasion—the launch of a groundbreaking cultural exchange program with an alien race far more technologically advanced than us. Meeting the Venorians in person for the first time was fascinating. I feel like I'm getting this much closer to my ultimate objective of building third generation spaceships that will allow us to travel to distant planets. I should be buzzing with excitement. Yet this evening has been purgatory.

All night, I've discreetly kept my eye on Viva. She's been in the company of Ralph and Troy, seemingly having a good time. I thought I would be okay with being separate from her for the duration of this reception. Our relationship is private. I don't need anybody poking their noses into it. As soon as we're out of here, we'll change into casual clothes then board a ship returning to Earth. I'll have her come to my sleep pod like before and hold her close while we sleep. She's mine, even if the world doesn't know it.

But fuck, I'm not okay. It's galling, not being able to acknowledge her. I want her proudly beside me, not on the other side of the room, pretending there is nothing between us. When Pravol called her my mate, I had felt a thrill. For a split second, I had wanted to shout to the world that yes, Viva was mine, and to draw her to me close. Then of course, Troy stepped in to deny it, telling everyone Viva was my massage therapist, not my mate. I had nearly wanted to throttle him. Instead, I had worked to keep a bland expression on my face, and made sure to look at anyone but Viva. If my eyes had met hers at that point, there's no guarantee I would have kept my control.

For the rest of the evening, I've followed her movements with my eyes, shifting my stance so I'm always keeping her within view. I saw her walk to the bathroom with a female acquaintance she'd met, then her short encounter with Shuban on the way out. I'm glad she's had a chance to meet the Venorians. I know she's been just as curious about them as I have. And then a short while ago, she began to make her way back towards where Ralph is standing. That's when that shitbag, Lucas Rivera, waylaid her. I watch now, my hands in fists, as he talks to her. Whatever he's saying is making her uncomfortable. Her stance is stiff. She keeps glancing down at her feet. What the fuck is going on?

A moment later, he puts a hand on her arm to stop her from walking away from him. I see red. Discretion be damned. Interrupting Ambassador Garcia, I mutter, "Excuse me," and stalk towards where that asshole is bothering Viva. I reach them just as I hear her telling him to remove his hand from her arm. In a fury, I spit out, "You heard what the lady said. Take your fucking hand off her now."

Rivera sees me and the raging expression on my face must convince him I'm not to be messed with. His hands come up in a mock surrender. "Now, now, Tobias. There's no need for this. I only wanted to persuade Viva to give me one of her famous sensual healing treatments. I hear she's one of the best. I'm even willing to pay double the usual rate. Perhaps you could put in a good word for me."

Is this asshole for real? My fury is now off the scale. I grip Viva around the waist and whisper into her ear, "Go to Ralph now." She hesitates. "Now, Viva." With a slight nod, she pivots and makes her way to my assistant. Now I turn my attention to the lowlife in front of me. My eyes narrow. "Let me make something crystal clear. You do not ever talk to Viva again. You do not ever approach her or her place of business for an appointment. And do not think of ever repeating to anyone this conversation we've had just now. Cross me and I will crush you like an ant. Got it?"

His face a notch paler, he nods.

"Now fucking get out of my face," I hiss. He doesn't need to be told twice. The fucking runt beats a hasty retreat. I watch him leave and take some deep calming breaths. Then I take out my communicator and message Viva.

Me: Baby, that man will never bother you again. I fixed it. You ok?

Viva: Yes.

Me: We'll leave soon. Get Ralph to make your excuses in five minutes and head back to the room.

Viva: Ok.

I put my communicator back in my pocket, feeling eyes on me. Some busty blonde is fluttering her eyelashes at me. I don't have time for this shit. Casting her a withering look, I march back to the group of people I had been with. As if I had never walked off, I resume the conversation, and they are all too polite to mention my sudden absence. I watch, a few minutes later, as Viva and Ralph make their way out to their transport. Time for me to make a move too. I catch Sven's eye and nod. Silently, he comes to stand behind me, while Yuri scouts the room ahead. I make my excuses and leave the reception.

Less than ten minutes later, I walk into the room we're staying in. "Viva!" I call out. She emerges from the connecting door to her own set of rooms, already changed into casual pants and a sweater. "Come here, girl," I growl. In an instant, she's in my arms, and the constriction in my chest eases as I breathe easy for the first time in several hours. I hold her to me tight, caressing the soft strands of her hair. She pulls away finally to look up at me, a question in her eyes. In answer, I ask, "You know when you once said I have the power to click my fingers and crush you like an ant?"

She nods. "Yes?"

"Well, I used that power today to warn Rivera. He ever comes near you again, I will crush him."

She gives a relieved smile. "I'm glad. That guy is just so sleazy. The way he asked me for a treatment with a salacious look on his face. Ugh!" She shudders.

I grit my teeth. "He won't bother you again."

"What about the rest of it? When Pravol let slip that I'm your mate?"

"I don't think that will be a problem. What I want to know is how the fuck the guy sussed we're together."

Her eyes gleam with excitement. "I'll tell you why, and you won't believe it. The Venorians are a telepathic race. When he put his forehead to mine, he read what was in my mind."

I park this revelation to one side for a minute to ask, "Just what the fuck was in your mind?"

She starts to speak, then stops, then starts again hesitantly. "I was thinking how big and sexy that guy was, and that it was a good thing I'm already yours."

"Goddamn right you are," I say, and kiss her. God I love the feel of her soft lips. And the taste of her. I deepen the kiss, letting my tongue slide in to her mouth. I'm rock hard with need. My hands fall to her ass, pushing her into my groin.

"Do we have time?" she asks breathlessly when I finally release her lips.

"If we're quick." I pull her towards the bed. "Lean your elbows down and stick your ass out for me, baby," I instruct. She's quick to do what I say. "Good girl," I grunt as I slip my hands inside the waist of her pants and pull them down, together with her panties. She steps out of them quickly. Just as rapidly, I shed my formal pants and briefs, then I'm palming my aching cock. "Hard and fast, baby," I warn.

"Give it to me," she breathes.

Without further preliminaries, I enter her lush pussy and bury myself in her heat. This is heaven. No other word for it.

"Ready for me?" I ask, on the edge of my control.

"Ready."

I plough into her, hard. Then I pull back and do it again. Fuck it feels good. I bring my hand to her clit just as I begin a punishing rhythm of thrusts, deep as I can go. "You gonna fucking come for me?" I demand as I piston into her.

"I-I..." she moans. "I'm close."

So am I, baby, so am I. "Come, Viva!" I thunder. And like the good girl she is, her pussy convulses around my cock. *Thank fuck.* A moment later, I'm pulsing my release into her. When I'm done, I rest my head on the small of her back and get my breath back. I recall what she said just now about the Venorians. "What makes you think they're telepathic?" I ask, resuming the conversation as if we hadn't just had a mind-blowing fuck. Slowly, I ease myself out of her and watch my cum leak out of her in satisfaction.

She turns around and sits up on the edge of the bed. "It's Martha who told me. She's one of the candidates for the exchange program who didn't make it through to the final list. When Shuban put his forehead to hers, she sensed what he was doing, and then he admitted it, saying he'd never before met a human that could do that."

I take her hand and lead her to the bathroom, all the while considering what she said. "That does explain their curious greeting ritual," I say as I grab hold of a wash cloth and bring it under the tap. I wring it dry and lean down to wipe the mess I've made of Viva. When I straighten up, her hands come to my shirt, undoing the fastenings. She helps me take off the rest of my clothes and takes them through to the bedroom while I quickly relieve myself and wash.

When I rejoin her, she's got my lounge pants and sweater out of the bag for me. I drop a kiss of thanks on her lips, then get myself dressed. I check my communicator. We need to be out in two minutes. "Ready, baby?"

"I'm ready."

"Then let's go home."

Chapter 18

Viva

Once our ship docks back on Earth, I get on a waiting drone that takes me back to Mom's house. Tobias and Ralph leave together with his bodyguards in another drone. "I'll see you Tuesday," he whispers to me before he gets into it.

In the drone, I sit back, my eyes half closed. The spaceship lag seems worse on the return journey than on the outgoing one. I'm bone tired, not even having the energy to check the notifications on my communicator. We land outside Mom's front door, and I climb out wearily. Pressing my wrist to the lock de-activator, I open the door and walk in, calling out, "Mom, Joe, I'm home!"

Two seconds later, Joe barrels into me like a dynamo. "Hey," I say, gathering him into my arms. "I missed you."

"Missed you too," comes his muffled voice.

Mom rounds the corner and looks at me in concern. "You look exhausted, honey."

"I am. Just need to get home, have a bath and get to sleep. You ready, Joe?"

"Yeah," he replies.

"Then let's go." I give Mom a quick hug. "I'll fill you in about it all tomorrow."

"You get some rest, and we'll talk in the morning," she says reassuringly.

A minute later, we're out the door and walking the block down to my apartment. We're about halfway there when I begin to notice the number of cars and drones on the street, and a crowd of people outside my building. What's going on? My sleepy mind cannot work out what it could be, so I carry on walking towards them. A few yards from home, someone in the crowd takes notice of me. "There she is!" he shouts.

Suddenly, I'm surrounded by a web of people calling out questions and snapping video footage.

"Is it true you're dating Tobias Moore?"

"When did you start dating?"

"Is Tobias Moore the father of your child?"

"Did Tobias Moore get into a fight with Lucas Rivera over you?"

I'm slow on the uptake, my exhaustion making my reflexes sluggish. Beside me, Joe is crying, "Momma, make them go away! They're scaring me." That spurs me out of my stupor.

"Get out of our way!" I shout, holding Joe tight by the hand as I push my way through the crowd to get to my front door. In a moment, I get it to open and we go in, closing it shut behind us.

"Momma, why are they here?" wails Joe.

"I don't know, sweet boy, but I'll get them to leave as soon as I can." I get my communicator and instruct Athena to close all the window blinds. "Athena, lights on," I then instruct. With that done, the clamor from outside is shut out. "Go brush your teeth and get your PJs," I tell Joe. Thankfully, he does as I ask. As soon as he's out of earshot, I call Tobias. He answers on the first ring.

"Viva—"

But I interrupt him angrily. "Tobias, there are hundreds of reporters camped outside my house. They asked all kinds of questions about you and me, and they made Joe cry."

"Fuck, I'm so sorry. I think a reporter overheard my altercation with Rivera and leaked the story. I had no idea this was going to happen."

"Well it has and now, you need to make it stop. I don't care what you do, but get those fucking reporters away from me and my family. Do it now, Mr All Powerful."

"I'm on it, baby."

"You heard what I said? I don't want a single reporter outside my door when I come out in the morning. Call the dogs off me and my son. Do whatever it takes."

He looks pale and ragged, but I'm out of sympathy at this moment. "Understood," he responds and ends the call.

I go find Joe and help him get ready for bed. Then I read to him until he falls asleep in my arms. Carefully, I carry him to his bed and settle him under the covers. I stand gazing at him in slumber for several minutes before I go take a hot shower and put on my nightshirt. In bed, I check my communicator one last time. I go to the news sites for the latest stories and find what I'm looking for. There's a press release from Tobias stating that he and I are not in anything other than a working relationship, and asking the press to respect my privacy. The press release goes on to reveal that Tobias has been secretly dating the artist Gefalda for the last three months, but that they're now ready to go public with their relationship. There's lots of pictures of this Gefalda, who of course, is tall and perfectly beautiful.

Realistically, I know this can't be true. It must be a lie, made up to convince the press to lay off me. When would he even had had the time to date this other woman when for the past six weeks, he's spent his evenings with me, either in person or via his communicator. As if on cue, it rings with an incoming from Tobias.

"Hey," I say, picking up.

"You saw the press release?"

"Yeah."

His reddened eyes plead with me. "None of it is true. You know that."

I nod. "I know."

"The only way to get them off your back was to put them onto another target. Gefalda is happy to do this, and she'll get well compensated for her troubles."

I sniff and realize my eyes are not quite dry. "Will you be dating her?" My voice comes out as a croak.

"Only in pretense, never for real."

"But you'll have to be seen out in public with her."

"Yes."

I'm silent, steeling myself for what needs to be said. We both speak at the same time.

"Tobias—"

"Viva—"

Then we stop. Tobias nods to me. "You go first."

I let out a deep breath and start again. "Tobias, this thing between us. It has to end now. I can't be dating you either in secret or in public. I'm sorry."

"Viva, give it a little time and the media interest will die down," he says in an urgent voice.

"Only to resurrect itself the minute a hint of us being together leaks out again. Long term, this is just not going to work. We've been kidding ourselves all these weeks, thinking it could."

"Every problem has an answer," he grits out. "Trust me, Viva. I'm going to find a way for us to work."

But there isn't a way. Frustration infuses my voice as I reply, "I can't ever expose my son to those media vultures again. I'm sorry, Tobias. I just can't, even though it hurts to let you go."

"Don't let me go! Baby, hold on for just a little more, and I promise I'll find a way", he pleads.

But I'm shaking my head, exhaustion and misery catching up with me. The tears are now rolling down my cheeks. "I'm sorry," I say again, my voice thick with emotion. "I have to go. Bye now." I end the call and put my communicator on privacy mode. Then I get under the covers and try to get some sleep.

Chapter 19

Viva

Tobias keeps to his word. In the morning, all the reporters are gone. Once I de-activate the privacy mode on my communicator, I find several messages from him.

Tobias: Baby, the reporters won't bother you again. I'm so sorry this happened. Please forgive me.

Tobias: Call me in the morning. We need to talk.

Tobias: I can't let you go, Viva. We'll make this work, I promise.

I glance at my son. Joe is happily playing in his virtual play space. My heart heavy, I call Tobias.

"Hey," I say as he picks up.

"Baby, you and Joe alright?"

I give a faint smile. "Yeah, we're doing okay. Thanks for calling off the mob."

His lips thin. "They won't bother you again, Viva. I've made sure each and every one of the reporters that were camped outside your door know that I will make it my personal business to destroy them if they approach you or Joe again."

"Thanks, Tobias."

"Viva, about us—"

I stop him there. "There can be no us."

He narrows his eyes. "I disagree, but let me just ask you a simple question. If it weren't for the bodyguards following me everywhere and the media attention, would you be willing to be with me?"

I huff out a frustrated breath. "That's a pointless question. You are never going to be an ordinary man living an ordinary life. There are always going to be people interested in what you're doing and wanting something from you, be it money or favors. Me and Joe could never walk down the block with you to eat a quiet meal at the local diner without being stared at or followed or pictures taken of us. You are who you are, and you can't change that."

He looks at me intently. "What if I could? Would you be with me then?"

I nearly growl in my exasperation. "Tobias, stop. Why torture ourselves with what ifs?"

"Because I'm the master of turning what ifs into reality. Now answer the question. Would you be with me then?"

I let out a long, defeated breath. "You know I would."

His smile is irritatingly smug. "Challenge accepted, Viva."

We end the call shortly after that. Mom comes round later in the morning, and I fill her in on all that's happened. When I'm done, she holds out her arms and gives me a big hug. One is never too old for comforting hugs from moms. She strokes my hair gently and says, "It's going to be alright, Viva. Whatever happens, you're strong and you have your family." Then she adds, "But I wouldn't write Tobias off completely. The man obviously cares for you, and he seems determined to do whatever it takes to make things right. Wait and see how it plays out."

I sigh. "I know he thinks he can do this, but he can't change who he is. He doesn't have it in his DNA to be the ordinary guy next door."

"Is that what you really want?"

I think about it. "No, not really. I fell in love with the extraordinary man that he is. I just don't want the attention that comes with it."

Mom releases me and sits back in her chair. After a thoughtful pause, she says, "For what it's worth, I think you've done the right thing, putting a break on the relationship. As the situation stands now, it's untenable for you and Joe. But if Tobias is as determined to fix it as he sounds, then I wouldn't be surprised if he comes up with some kind of solution. Wait and see what he decides to do, and then reassess. And just remember, you might need to meet him halfway on this and find an acceptable compromise. Nothing worthwhile is ever easy. You know that."

I take a sip of coffee, before replying, "I do, but I have to put Joe's wellbeing above everything in my considerations."

"Of course you do. Now how about you show us what gifts you have brought back from your travels."

"Oh dang!" In the haze of my exhaustion and the ensuing drama, I'd totally forgotten about them. I stand, promising, "I'll get them now."

The rest of the day is quiet and uneventful. I venture out in the early afternoon with Joe to get some groceries, looking left and right to see if there are any reporters about. Thankfully, I don't see any suspicious activity. That evening, after Joe has gone to bed, I settle down in my malleable armchair to read the latest novel I've downloaded. I half expect a call from Tobias. We've gotten so used to being together every evening, virtually or otherwise. By ten o'clock, I realize that's not going to happen tonight. Of course it isn't. Didn't I tell him we were over? I'm disappointed nonetheless.

Monday, I take Joe to school then head off to work at Sensual Healing. I'm not surprised when, on walking through the lobby door, I'm accosted by Loni, wanting a private talk with me. Warily, I follow her to her office. She goes to sit behind her imposing desk and observes me with steely eyes. "Viva," she says. "I've had quite a few calls from reporters this weekend, asking questions about you and Tobias. Of course, I told them that, as per our stated policy, master healers do not involve themselves in personal relationships with clients. Now I'll ask you the question and I want your truthful answer. Did you cross that line?"

I squirm in my seat, not knowing what to say. To admit that I have had a personal relationship with Tobias will result in my instant dismissal. I know Loni. She has zero tolerance for her rules being broken. And yet lying does not come easily to me. In the end, I settle for a statement as close to the truth as possible. "I have conducted my treatment sessions with the utmost professionalism," I tell her.

She studies me for several moments. "I see," she says dryly. Then she sits forward, steepling her hands. "Viva, I have worked hard to build up the reputation of this establishment. We do not engage in sex work here. All our master healers work to the highest professional standards. And although you have been one of my best healers and Tobias Moore is a major client, I will not hesitate to terminate your contract here if I have any evidence that you are conducting yourself in a way that contravenes my rules."

I look down at my lap as I murmur, "I understand."

"Good. That's all for now. I'll let you go get ready for your next client."

I stand quickly and make a hasty retreat. Another good reason why Tobias and I need to be over, I think as I walk down the corridor to my treatment room. I can't afford to lose this job.

The week passes slowly. I get back to my normal routine, working during the day then having quiet evenings in with Joe. From Tobias, I hear nothing. I appreciate that he's respecting my wishes. There's no halfway house to breaking up. You're either together or you're not. I miss him, there's no doubt about it. My evenings are long and lonely. I wonder about how he's doing. Has he reverted to being Mr Grumpy again? As the week progresses, my thoughts zoom in on one thing. Friday, six pm, my next appointment with Tobias. He hasn't cancelled it, so I assume it's still on. And when he arrives, I am going to act professional, come what may. My job is on the line.

At five to six on Friday, I get the treatment room ready and start the bath. At one minute to six, I get notified that Tobias has arrived. Thank God! I hadn't realized quite how much I had worried that he wouldn't show up. Nervously, I wipe my damp palms on the fabric of my tunic and go open the door. He stands there, flanked by his bodyguards. "Good evening, Mr Moore," I manage to say.

"Hello, Viva," he says, his voice deep and smooth, just as I remember it. He brushes past me into the room. I shut the door and lean against it. My gaze follows his path to the spa room, where he's already dropping his clothes. A moment later, he's lowering himself into the bath. I'm still frozen by the door until his voice like whiplash calls out an order, "Come here."

My feet take me to the spa room. I pause at the threshold. "Yes, Mr Moore?" I'm going to do professional even if it kills me.

"Sit with me while I bathe."

"Yes, sir." Stiffly, I walk over to the chair and position myself on it, back ramrod straight. I expect him to say something, but he doesn't. He simply closes his eyes, and rests his head on the bath pillow. We stay like this for several minutes.

I study him surreptitiously, drinking in the sight of his beautifully masculine face, the strong jaw, firm lips and the powerful arms resting on the side of the bath, smooth bronze skin peppered with fine dark hair. His voice when he speaks, takes me by surprise. Very softly, he asks, "How have you been?"

"Good, thank you," I murmur. "And you?"

"Just peachy," he responds with an ironic twist to his lips. He pins me with his gray-eyed gaze. "Let's try that again, Viva, and with the truth this time. How have you been?"

I shrug. "Okay, I guess."

He nods his head. "A more honest response than 'good'. I've been okay too, though much more of a grump because I've missed you."

I don't know what to say to that. Good? Instead, I decide to tell him about my conversation with Loni last Monday. His face hardens as I recount what was said. I finish by saying, "So you see how important it is that we keep our relationship professional from now on. I can't be losing my job over this."

"You won't," he grits. "I've told you before that you need never worry about your job."

"But I do, no matter what you say. So, Tobias, please can we keep things on the level here?"

He reaches out his hand to me, palm up. Uncertainly, I lean forward and place my hand in his. "Viva," he says, looking intently at me. "I respect your work. When I'm here, I'll play by the rules. But I want you to know something. We are not done. I know I have things to do my end to make it right for you, and I'm on it. When the time's right, I'm coming for you."

A shiver of anticipation runs through me at his words, but all I say is, "Okay." He releases my hand and stands, water streaming down his toned body. My breath hitches. Why does he have to be so fucking beautiful? Awkwardly, I get up and make my way back to the treatment room, busying myself with lighting candles until he's lying face down on the massage bed. Then, taking a deep breath in, I begin the treatment.

Chapter 20

Viva

Another dreary week passes. If anything, it's worse than the last. Being without Tobias is like eating bland processed bread rather than a sourdough full of flavor—tolerable but dull and drab. What makes it worse is goddamn Valentine's Day, which means I get bombarded with media trying to sell me a cornucopia of unnecessary things to mark this supposed romantic day. No, I do not require personalized Love Hearts candies. Nor do I want his and hers "I heart _" socks. I might have considered the box of heart-shaped praline chocolates if it weren't for the exorbitant price. Let's face it. Nobody whose heart has just been broken wants to be around for Valentine's Day. I wish I could just hibernate and not wake up until late spring, when at least the sun would shine to brighten up my days.

And throughout the wearisome week, one thing and one thing only sustains me. Friday, six pm, my appointment with Tobias. Last week, I gave him a highly professional and satisfying treatment. For an hour, I worshipped his body with my hands and made it my business to give him an exquisitely blissful experience. At the end, he thanked me politely and let me go. I wake this Friday morning with a sense of anticipation absent from previous days. I wash, dress, have breakfast with Joe then take him to school, trying to ignore the big hearts on the billboard.

Afterwards, I walk back home. There's a small box sitting in my entryway when I let myself in through the door. I pick it up curiously. It's plain with nothing on the label except for my name and address. I open it and look inside. I find a heart-shaped pastel pink box with my name artfully inscribed on the top. I untie the satin ribbon and open the box. It contains heart-shaped praline chocolates, hand-made to a traditional Swiss recipe. A small note drops out of the box. I pick it up and read, "My heart beats for you. T"

I can't help but smile at the sweet, romantic gesture. I type the words "Thank You" and send them as a message to Tobias. He promptly messages back, "Enjoy! xxx". I sample one of the chocolate hearts and yes, I do enjoy. So much so that I eat another, then another. I force myself to stop, putting the box away in the kitchen, then get myself to work. I power through the list of morning appointments, finally stopping for my lunchbreak at one pm. Leaving my last client to get dressed at leisure, I make my way to the staff quarters and wash my hands thoroughly. I'm just about to open my locker and take out my sandwich when Suri comes in, bearing a medium-sized cardboard box. "This just came for you," she says. I take it from her, intrigued, but wait until she's out of the room before I open it.

Inside is a freshly baked bagel with cream cheese and generous layers of smoked salmon. Beside it, in another small box, is a heart-shaped strawberry tart. There's another note, again handwritten in Tobias's distinctive script, "For my favorite person, some of her favorite foods. I noticed how much you enjoyed the smoked salmon at the reception, and I know you love strawberries. Enjoy your lunch. Can't wait to see you tonight. T xxx".

I take a photo of them on my communicator, then send Tobias a message: "You're spoiling me." Again, his answer is immediate. "You deserve it and more. Enjoy it, baby." Carefully, I pick up the bagel and take my first bite. Yum. That smoked salmon is so tender, it melts in the mouth.

Soon, I'm taking another bite and then another. It's not long before the bagel is consumed. I drink some water and then attack the strawberry tart, which is achingly delicious. I pat my full stomach. That was rather more than I usually eat at lunchtime, but oh so good. I don't linger too long after I've eaten. I have two more clients to see this afternoon before it's time for Tobias. With a happy sigh, I stand and head back to my treatment room to begin preparations. Just as I do, I hear the bleep of a notification. Checking my communicator, I see there's a new press report about Tobias. Call me foolish, but I've set Athena to notify me anytime a new story about Tobias comes out.

I scroll to it now and read, my face creasing in a frown. The headline says, "The world's richest man divests himself of half his fortune". Intrigued, I read the report. According to this, Tobias has set up a new charitable foundation and endowed it with half his fortune, a reported $2.5 trillion. Few details have yet to emerge about this charitable foundation, who will manage it or what its focus will be. However, the divestment means that Tobias Moore has now dropped down the rich list dramatically, no longer topping it and not even placing in the top hundred anymore. *Curious.* Why would he do this? I go back to work, thinking about it, though I make a special effort to keep my focus on each client.

Just after five thirty, I finish with my last client and head over to the staff quarters to take a short break. That's where Loni finds me, some minutes later. "Viva," she says. "Mr Moore's assistant has just been in touch to say he's unable to come to you today for his treatment." My heart sinks but flutters again when I hear what she has to say next. "However, he would like you to go to him. His drone will come pick you up in five minutes. You won't need to bring anything with you, I'm told, as everything has been fully set up for your treatment." She pauses, fixing me with glacial eyes. "I hope you have not forgotten our earlier conversation about keeping things professional, nor the consequences if that professionalism slips."

"I haven't. I'm sticking to the rules."

"Good, keep it that way." She leaves me then without another word. Quickly, I start gathering my belongings from my locker. I put my coat and scarf on before hurrying to call an elevator. I reach the rooftop just as the drone makes its landing. My pulse racing, I walk towards it and climb aboard. Inside the drone, a surprise awaits me.

Tobias is there, and wordlessly, he hands me a large pink envelope. I take it from him, saying humorously, "What's with the pink today?"

Very seriously, he responds, "I believe it is the color most associated with Valentine's Day. However, if you object to it, I'll make sure to give you gifts in another color next year at Valentine's." He nods to the envelope. "Open it."

I take a seat beside him and tear open the pink envelope, which I see is embossed with hearts. "Cute," I say. I take out the card inside. It has a familiar picture on the front. It's a depiction of the mural at his house, the one where two soulmates are holding hands and facing the world as one. I open the card to read the message.

Dear Viva,

The more I see this mural, the more I realize it's us. You and me (with Joe) facing the world. I know that if all hell were to break loose tomorrow, there'd be only one person I'd want by my side and that's you. So, if my massive fortune is the impediment to us being together, then I'll gladly give it away. You'll maybe have seen today that I have donated half my fortune to a charitable foundation. If that is still not enough, I will donate even more. At least I'm no longer the world's richest man or even in the top hundred. I would like you to help me lead the foundation and decide what kind of projects it should spend money on, but only if you want to.

Tonight, before we have our treatment—which I will never want to miss—I'm taking you to see the new home I have bought for us. I hope one day, you and Joe will live there with me. Don't say no yet. Keep an open mind.

Happy Valentine's Day

Tobias xxx

I put the card down with trembling hands. "Where are you taking me?" I ask.

He puts the card to one side and takes one of my hands in his. "You'll see. Did you enjoy your lunch today?"

I smile. "If the speed at which it was consumed is evidence, then I would say yes." I lean my head against his shoulder, saying, "Thank you, Tobias. All these little gifts from you. They made my day."

He puts an arm around me, chuckling. "Good. And the best is still to come." We stay like this throughout the short journey, not saying very much. At our descent, I look out the window, trying to see through the darkness to where we are landing. "Patience, Viva. You'll find out soon enough," says Tobias laughingly.

The drone comes to a stop, and the doors open automatically. Tobias stands and holds my hand as we step out into the cold February night. I look about me in surprise. We're outside Mom's house in Brooklyn. I turn to him, perplexed. "Why are we at Mom's?" I ask.

He smiles enigmatically. "We can visit your mom later, but that is not our destination tonight. I would like you to cast your eyes on the house next door."

I do as he says, looking towards the house to the left of Mom's. It's a red brick property with a neatly landscaped front yard. I know it's owned by Mr and Mrs Nazarian, an Armenian-American couple with two grown kids. More puzzled than ever, I say, "I'm looking at it. It's Mr and Mrs Nazarian's house."

"It was," replies Tobias. "As of yesterday afternoon, it became mine. The Nazarians were happy to accept a cash offer well above the market value of their house, with which they plan to move closer to their eldest son in Arizona." He turns to me. "I thought you might like to continue living close to your mom, and you can't get any closer than next door. Come on, let's have a look inside." He takes my hand and leads me up the front steps, deftly unlocking the door with his wristband.

I've been struck speechless ever since the beginning of his speech. Now, as I step over the threshold and take in the empty rooms before me, I splutter, "I can't believe this!"

"Believe it. This is my new home, and I very much want it to be your home too, but no pressure." He walks to the front living room and looks around. "This house has good bones. The rooms are airy and spacious. With a little loving care, this could be a lovely home."

I shake my head. "How can you say that when I know your current home looks nothing like this."

He shrugs. "I thought we would keep it for now as a vacation home—maybe the place we spend our summers at. But for our everyday life, I think this place will do just fine. There are four good sized bedrooms and two and a half bathrooms. More than enough space for the three of us."

I'm still trying to process this new reality. Will this solve our problem? I try to think it through. "Even if you move here," I say, "you'll still be pursued by the media."

"No," he says flatly, "I won't. Firstly, I will put out a statement that I plan to retire from all public life. I will not be attending any more glitzy premieres or charitable auctions. And though I will continue to take an active interest in my business, I will no longer be its public face. I think it's high time Ralph got a promotion, don't you?"

I look doubtful. "The press would still come after you."

"Maybe at first, but attention will die down as they see me live an ordinary life. There can be very little interest for readers in seeing reports of a man walking to the local diner or going to buy groceries. In any case, reporters found to be harassing us will soon learn the hard way why that is not a good idea."

I search in my mind for other reasons why this won't work. "What about security and your bodyguards?" I look out the window. "Where are they, by the way?"

"They've been fired. Well, more like transferred to other duties. I won't be needing bodyguards following me everywhere. Firstly because I'm no longer going to be a high profile person in the media, and secondly because I no longer have the kind of wealth that might trigger an elaborate kidnapping attempt." He pulls me to him, and I go willingly. Kissing the top of my head, he adds, "That's not to say I've ditched all security measures. This house is going to be kitted with a top of the range system, and I'm trialling out a personal security upgrade to our communicators that will scan our surroundings whenever we're out and warn us of any suspicious activity."

He draws back a little to look at me. "So, Viva, I once asked you a question. If it weren't for the bodyguards following me everywhere and the media attention, would you be willing to be with me? At the time, you said you would. So now that I've dealt with both those issues, baby, will you be with me? Date me openly, live with me, be my partner in life, whichever you prefer."

I want to say yes, but there's one more problem. "If I date you openly, I lose my job."

"Ah," he says, with a mysterious smile. "I've thought of that too. Now we come to the next part of your Valentine's gift." He takes my hand and leads me outside again. He points to the small house on the opposite side of the street. "I decided it's time, Viva, that you struck out on your own. I've not liked the way you've been treated at Sensual Healing, and I think you can make a go of things in your own right. I'd bet most of your clients there would come to you if you set up your own practice."

I gaze at him suspiciously. "Tobias, what have you done?"

With a cryptic expression, he says, "Come see." Briskly, he walks me across the street and up the house's front steps. Hanging from its door is a large bouquet of pink roses arranged in the shape of a heart. He unlocks the door with his wrist band and leads me inside. On a side table lies another large pink envelope which he hands over to me, saying, "I bought this house for you, Viva. Here are the deeds in your name. It's yours to do whatever you want with it, but I'm thinking you might want to use it as your new place of business. Come take a look."

I'm beginning to shake all over. This is too much. Unbelievable. Magical. Tobias pauses and looks at me in concern, rubbing comforting hands down my arms. "You okay?"

"I-I don't know. This is so much to take in."

He smiles reassuringly. "It's all good, but let's take a pause and just hold each other. Come here, baby girl." He pulls me into his embrace and I nestle there, trying to let it all sink in. In typical Tobias fashion, he's gone and solved the conundrum of how we can be together. Why should I put up any more road blocks when all I want is this life together he's proposing? All at once, I'm awash with love for this magnificent man. I need to tell him.

Looking up into his solemn gray eyes, I blurt, "I love you, and I want to be with you."

Tenderly, he replies, "I love you too. Will you move in and live with me?"

"Let's take it slow," I say with a tremulous smile. "Let Joe get used to the idea of us being together before we make the big move."

He nods. "Then that's what we'll do. You ready to come see the rest of the house?"

"I'm ready."

He takes me by the hand and leads me to a large room, pleasantly furnished with a malleable couch and armchairs, set around a coffee table. "I thought this space could be the waiting room for your clients when they arrive," he says. "For your safety, I'll have Sven work at the main reception area—that's going to be his new job from now on, keeping you safe. Any client cause you hassle, Sven will deal with them."

"What about poor Yuri?" I quip.

He smiles. "Don't worry, I've got him working on setting up and monitoring the security for our new house. You ready to see upstairs?"

I grin. "I'm ready."

He takes me up the stairs to a door which he opens, revealing a room painted a pretty pastel peach, set up with a massage bed and all the equipment I will need for a treatment. I barely have time to take it all in before he's moving on to a connecting door that opens into the most beautifully appointed spa room I have ever seen. I walk in and run my hand over the smooth porcelain of the bath tub, admiring it. All the while, Tobias watches me. I turn to him now, my voice not quite steady as I say, "It's perfect."

He lets out a long breath, looking relieved. "Happy Valentine's Day, Viva."

I go to him and put my arms around his waist. "Happy Valentine's Day, Tobias."

He bends his head to kiss me. "Now, how about that sensual healing treatment I've been waiting for all week?"

"Coming right up," I smile. "Let me start the spa bath while you undress." He releases me and I turn to tap on the display button for a hot bath. Water immediately begins to fill the tub. On the side, I see a jar of Sensual Healing bath salts, from which I pour a handful into the steaming water.

Observing me, Tobias muses, "In time, you'll have to market your own brand of bath salts but for now, we'll use these." He's already got his shirt off, revealing that beautiful chest tattoo I love so much. Next his shoes, pants and briefs come off until he's standing, gloriously naked. I only have a short moment to admire his perfection before he's letting himself into the bath with a happy sigh. "Oh that feels good," he breathes.

I leave him a short while to hang my coat and hat on a convenient peg by the door, wash my hands, and then start getting myself ready for this treatment. I promise myself it's going to be the best Tobias has ever had. I hear him step out of the bath and next moment, he's striding into the treatment room, a happy smile on his face. "I'm so ready for this," he says with glee. "Gonna make it good for me?"

"The very best," I assure him.

He settles himself face down. I drizzle some oil on his back and begin.

Epilogue

Tobias

One year later

I wake to the feel of Viva's soft body wrapped around me and the sound of her even breathing. For a long moment, I just drift in that happy state of semi-sleep, enjoying her closeness. I know I'll have to get up soon, as there's important things to be done, but I linger for a few minutes more.

It's been seven months since Viva and Joe moved into this house with me, and many more since I've known that I want her to be my wife. Today, our Valentine's Day anniversary, is the day when I'll get down on my knees and ask the question. I have it all planned out. Starting with a delicious breakfast in bed.

Gently, I disengage myself from Viva and tiptoe to the bathroom, where I quickly wash and get dressed. Then I'm letting myself out of our bedroom door and heading two doors down to Joe's room. As I look in on him, he's stirring awake. I go sit on the edge of his bed and say softly, "Ready, Joe?"

He sits up with a loud yawn. "Yeah, let's do this."

"Get yourself dressed and join me downstairs," I tell him.

"Okay."

I leave him to it and make my way down, checking my communicator. The delivery I'm expecting is two minutes away, which gives me just enough time to prepare the tray and pour the coffee. A notification bleep tells me it's here. I go to the front door and open it, taking two boxes from the delivery bot. By now, Joe has joined me and together, we tear open the boxes. One of them contains a beautifully arranged bouquet of red roses. I pluck one of the roses out and place it as artistically as I can on the tray.

Meanwhile, Joe is inspecting the contents of the other box. Inside is a selection of freshly baked pastries—croissants, brioches and several differently flavored muffins, together with some crusty rolls. "Wow, these smell good," he marvels.

"We'll soon get to eating them," I tell him. "Why don't you take out the pastry basket from the cupboard over there, and we can put the pastries in it." While he does that, I get the orange juice and the butter, adding them to the tray. "How does that look?" I ask Joe.

"Nice!" he says succinctly.

"Do you have the cards?" I ask.

He goes to get them from the drawer where we hid them yesterday and places them on the tray. I scan everything with my eyes, wondering if there's anything I've missed out. Cutlery! Quickly, I get some butter knives and napkins to add to the now heaving tray. I try to rearrange everything so it looks good. Satisfied, I turn to Joe. "Ready?"

"Ready."

I hand him the flower bouquet to carry and take the tray. "Let's go."

Viva

I COME AWAKE slowly, realizing I'm alone in the bed. Where's Tobias got to? A glance at the ceiling clock tells me it's only seven thirty. Just as I'm sitting up, there's a quick knock on the door. It opens to reveal Joe carrying flowers, and behind him, Tobias with a breakfast tray.

I grin. "Is that for me?"

"Yes, Momma. Just for you on Valentine's Day."

I clutch my chest. "Aww you guys." I take the flowers from Joe and drop a kiss on his cheek. "Thanks," I murmur.

Tobias comes in with the tray, placing it on the side table, which at the touch of a clever button, opens up into a breakfast table that can slide across the bed. He does just love to have these clever furniture gadgets. I look down at the contents of the tray, sniffing appreciatively. "This looks delicious, thank you."

He leans down to kiss me. "Open your cards first. This first one is from Joe."

Smiling at my son, I tear open the envelope and take out a card with a valentines themed design. "This is so pretty," I say.

"Read what it says inside," cries my son eagerly.

"Okay, I will." I open the card and read.

Dear Momma,

Happy Valentine's Day!

I love you lots.

P.S. Tobias wants to ask you something. I'd like it very much if you said yes.

"Thanks, sweet boy," I tell him, immensely touched. I lean over to give him another kiss. "I love you lots too."

Then I pick up the other envelope and tear it open, taking out the card, which has a gloriously cheesy pink heart design. Inside it says:

Dear Viva,

Our second Valentine's Day!

This last year we've had has been the happiest of my life. I know I want to spend the rest of it with you, my love, so please, pretty please, will you marry me?

I love you lots and lots and lots.

Tobias xxx

I look up to find Tobias kneeling by the bed and holding out to me a beautiful, unostentatious diamond ring. "Marry me, Viva," he says softly.

"Say yes!" encourages Joe.

I take the ring, admiring its lovely simplicity, and slip it on my finger. "Yes, I will," I tell the man I love.

Afterword

I hope you enjoyed this novella which I wrote especially to mark Valentine's Day. If you would like to read another Valentine's novella of mine, then do grab yourself a copy of **It's Always Been You**.

Please do also consider subscribing to my newsletter on **mmwakeford.substack.com** to get latest authorly news, book recommendations and exclusive extras, or check out my website, **mw-author.com**, for more in-depth information about my publications.

May I ask you for a small favour?

Reviews are the life blood of independent authors. Please could you help spread the word about this book by submitting a review on **Amazon**, **Goodreads** or any other book reader platform. Even a sentence or two makes a real difference for independent authors and helps other readers discover the book.

Thank you!

M.M. Wakeford

About the author

M.M. Wakeford lives with her husband and son in a London terraced house that gathers dust while she loses herself in her writing. A lifelong reader of romantic novels, she writes in many genres including contemporary, sci-fi and historical romance.

Her stories capture that heady feeling of falling in love, with emotionally rich characters whose journey to a happily ever after is lined with dilemmas, desire and difficult choices. If you're looking for a page turning romance with high emotion and a good dose of spice, you're in the right place.

To be the first to hear about new releases, sneak previews and exclusive extras, sign up for M.M. Wakeford's mailing list at <u>mw-author.com</u>.

Also by this author

IT'S ALWAYS BEEN YOU

I've been in love with Wilfred Barton-Browne for years.

Years of watching him from the sidelines. Years of pretending I don't notice the way he lights up a room, or how his rare, genuine smile makes my heart race. Years of being just his little sister's best friend.

He's a celebrated film producer—gorgeous, brilliant, always just out of reach. And I'm... me. Ordinary. Invisible.

Then comes Christmas Eve, and one mortifying accident changes everything. One moment where the careful distance between us shatters. Suddenly he's looking at me differently—like he's seeing me for the first time.

Maybe I've been looking at this all wrong. Maybe the man I thought saw me as nothing more than a familiar face has been seeing me all along.

Now Valentine's Day is around the corner, and the impossible is starting to feel achingly real.

*It's **Always Been You** is a tender, multicultural romance about finding the courage to reach for what your heart wants most.*

Tropes: Best Friend's Brother • Secret Crush • Opposites Attract • Sweet Closed-Door Romance

Praise for It's Always Been You:

"A lovely and heartwarming romance that sweetened my evening. I love a good contemporary romance novella and this one certainly hit all the good spots... I devoured this book whole and could not put it down." Lilith - Goodreads review

"OH WOW this was a great story. It was a page turner and the suspense was sweet... I was on the edge of my seat and I couldn't even put it down. The chemistry was captivating." Trina - Goodreads review

"This was a short read, and yet beautifully written. It felt like witnessing a love story of two people who met in their prime, and seeing them fall deeper in love as they grow old together." NiqueReads - Goodreads review

"I thought this was a super cute short read for Valentines Day. The writing was great and it was such a heartwarming story." Courtney - Goodreads review

"A very sweet, wholesome valentines novella with a sprinkle of spice!" Kirsty - Goodreads review

"This is exactly what it says: a sweet, heartwarming valentine romance." Leslie - Goodreads review

"A quick easy read that I enjoyed from the start." Noreen - Goodreads review

"A short but captivating novel that captivates with its simplicity. The writing is direct and effective, delivering a story that, although brief, keeps you hooked. A great story for those who like short books that are easy to read in one sitting." Lia - Goodreads review

"This was a cute novella perfect for a Valentine's Day read! I liked how the timeline was structured and the dual POV for the start of their relationship. Part of me wishes it had been longer, but I liked how much feeling and plot the author worked in at less than 100 pages!" Heather - Goodreads review

"What a sweet little Valentine's Day novella. This is a cute winter read… Wilfred is so sweet and such a gentleman. Karima's marble cake recipe at the end was such a sweet touch!" Nycole - Goodreads review

"I really enjoyed this heartwarming Valentine's Day romance… If you like romantic, quick reads about mature couples who still are very much in love after decades of marriage, you are sure to enjoy this book!" Marion - Goodreads review

KRANTOR'S MATE

One day, on a planet far from Earth, I meet my fated mate. The only problem is, he's in love with someone else.

Martha has enrolled on a six-month exchange program to the planet Ven, whose people have recently made first contact with Earth. Newly single and broke, Martha looks forward to this once-in-a-lifetime opportunity to find out more about the Venorians, an intriguing humanoid race of massive bronze-skinned people.

As the son and heir of the Kran, planet Ven's ruler, Krantor has four somars—men who are his lifelong bodyguards and companions. He loves them all dearly, but one of them, Prilor, he loves best of all. Krantor knows he's destined to meet his fated mate one day, but it's Prilor he wants to spend his days and nights with. And he certainly hadn't banked on his fated mate being a human!

Will Martha give up her life on Earth for a fated mate who already loves another? And what of the feelings she has developed for Shanbri, another of Krantor's somars?

Author's note: this is a standalone sci-fi romance with steam and spice aplenty, featuring FM, MM, and MFM relationships, and a guaranteed HEA for all.

Praise for Krantor's Mate:

"Trope busting. Loved it... M. M. Wakeford offers a completely new take on fated mates. With all the expectations that are set with a trope, the author blows it out of the water with her fabulous storytelling. I completely enjoyed this take on RH, fated mates, and deep-abiding love." ★★★★★ **Goodreads review**

"What a phenomenal read. The worlds, cultures, and species created were diverse and detailed. The characters were rich, vivid, and beautifully flawed. I went on such an emotional ride with this book." ★★★★★ **Goodreads review**

"An interesting and original approach to the reverse harem and fated mate tropes... Thought-provoking and provocative, with high heat throughout." ★★★★★ **Goodreads review**

*"I really enjoyed this book. Great world building... Lots of yummy steamy scenes to keep me happy, too. *wink*"* ★★★★★ **Goodreads review**

"This is a fantastic sci-fi romance with m/m mfm fm and mmmm relationships... I loved it and the characters and I highly recommend this book." ★★★★★ **Goodreads review**